MW01073709

Praise for Hillary Broome Novels

House of Cuts

A maniacal butcher, a journalist/teacher with a shameful secret, and a cigar-toting detective set the stage for this psychological thriller, the first in a series of Hillary Broome novels. Set in California's Central Valley, *House of Cuts* involves suspense, intrigue, and a burgeoning romance. My favorite things about this novel include the dialogue, the wonderful details, and its sense of place—from the lush walnut orchards of Morada, CA, to PriceCuts, what Gillam terms the "24/7 machine," the kind of superstore familiar to any modern reader. I also enjoyed the fact that eight of the fifty-one chapters are told from killer Melvin's point of view so that I was able to get a first-hand glimpse into his demented, mother-obsessed mind.

Candace Andrews, author of
High Tides: Wading Through Depression—Every Day

House of Dads

One if Gillam's strong virtues as a writer is her ability to enmesh you, the reader, in the many layered action of the story until you become that close and helpless bystander who must live every unspeakable thing out with the characters. Too bad about the hundred things and obligations with their gummy fingers on you. Too bad until the story is finished, for you are not free to return focus to your own life, not yet. When you close the book at last, it is with a sigh of relief and gratitude and satisfaction that YOU don't have to live out such things yourself as you and the characters have experienced together. Oh, but all will linger in your mind. And at the same time, you will already have an eye out for the next Hillary Broome adventure!

Zoe Keithley, author of
The Calling of Mother Adelli

HOUSE OF EIRE

A Hillary Broome Novel

June Gillam

Published by Gorilla Girl Ink, USA
ISBN 978-0-9858838-6-7

FOR OUR MOTHER,
GERALDINE PRICE SKALISKY ROBESON
WHO SANG "GALWAY BAY"
TO MY SISTERS AND ME

AUGUST 2014

In all of us there is a hunger, marrow-deep, to know our heritage, to know who we are and where we have come from. Without this enriching knowledge, there is a hollow yearning . . . and the most disquieting loneliness.

Alex Haley, *Roots*

PART I

Turning and turning in the widening gyre
The falcon cannot hear the falconer.

W. B. Yeats, "The Second Coming"

CHAPTER 1

SATURDAY MORNING IN LODI, CALIFORNIA

SUNLIGHT STREAMED through the window and roused Hillary. She lay sweating and still encased in the dream. *A cocoon had slipped over her feet and slid up the length of her body.*

Her heart clattered in her throat. She clawed at the top sheet bunched at her neck, groaned and threw back the covers. The mother nightmares. They were back. She sat at the edge of the bed, groggy and bent over, forearms pressed against her thighs, fingers folded, almost in prayer.

Ed's side was empty, and Claire was away on a sleepover.

Hillary padded downstairs in her damp nightgown. The valley heat was already heavy in the house—evaporating the sweat off her skin, drying her nightie.

As black brew dripped into Mr. Coffee, she stared out the kitchen window at row after row of grapevines rising from the dark soil. Why now? Her deadlines were over, it was time for vacation. While some people got migraines when the pressure let up, she had bad dreams.

Clutching a mug of French roast, she sat at the trestle table and stared at stacks of printouts. The piles had grown over the past months, plane tickets bought and tour reservations made. She was exhausted from mixing travel planning with writing to her publisher's tight deadlines. To distract herself from the dream's shadow, she started a final to-do list for this trip she needed so badly. Two weeks in Ireland sounded like heaven. If it came without dreams.

She flinched as the back door squeaked open and Ed came bounding in.

"You're up, Chickadee!" He bent to nuzzle the back of her neck. "And still in your nightie. Ummm." He slid his fingers under the straps of her gown and caressed her shoulder, then bent to brush his chin lightly against her arm. Her muscles let go, soothed by his tenderness.

He straightened. "Wish I could stay and play but on my way to a scene." He poured himself a cup of coffee. "City guys called us. A shooting near the festival grounds."

He set his Notre Dame mug down, reached for her hand and tapped the row of tiny emeralds in her wedding band. "We'll finally get there." He stroked her hand. "Earned our honeymoon."

She nodded. "Good thing that Gang Summit came along to help pay for it."

"I haven't told the others I'm mixing pleasure with business." He leaned to kiss her. "Don't want the ribbing I'd take."

She laughed and kissed him back. "And Roger's meeting us at the pub tonight with my paycheck. We're rich!"

He swigged down a gulp of coffee. "We're lucky he let us in on the income here, too," he said. He walked over to raise the window sash and take a deep breath of dusty air. "The grapes are looking good." He drained his coffee. "We'll be back in time for the Zinfandel harvest."

Hillary nodded, remembering when her publisher Roger had bought the acreage as an investment during the recession's low land prices. He'd let them run it with option to buy. One of the best parts was they'd been able to convert an outbuilding into a cottage for her old friend Sarah.

"We'll celebrate tonight, Chickadee." He rinsed out his cup and left.

Hillary stood at the open window and waved as he drove down the dirt road edging the rows of black grapes. She studied the dark fruit, plump and hanging low on the vines. In a few years they would mature into a bold red wine boasting poetic descriptions on labels—blackberry, anise and pepper notes. This year's crop looked promising, fed by the roots' life in the rich soil.

The dry heat of California's central valley began shouting its presence. Time to close up the house and turn on the AC. Hillary reached for the top half of the double-hung window. The paint was starting to peel on the wooden frame. The wavy glass refracted sunlight through in faint parallel ripples, flashing images from the dream into her mind's eye. One day she would dig for courage to go find her mother. Confront her and put to rest the nightmares. She was tired but afraid to risk going back to bed or even think of taking an afternoon nap. She slammed down the sash. Got to get busy.

CHAPTER 2

GALWAY, IRELAND

SEAMUS STOOD at the bottom of the stairwell and shouted up, "Ready for breakfast?"

"Please do not call to me while I am shifting gears." Bridget came running barefoot down the stairs, waving her hairbrush in the air. "You know I hate leaving after last night."

Sunbeams shot through the entry hall windows, striking her long black hair, tracing highlights he hadn't noticed before. He bent to brush his fingertips across her cheek and scissor a few strands of her dark tresses along their fall to her waist.

"No, sir, Mr. Shay. None of that now." She laughed and tapped her brush gently against his chest. "Plenty of that last night. Yes, I'll take a cup of your gorgeous coffee, if you please. Then off to my serious business." She pivoted on the red tile floor and ran back up the stairs, leaving the scent of roses in the air.

Seamus paused a second to inhale the fragrance before he returned to her tiny kitchen. *Shay.* Her nickname for him—another thing he loved about her American ways. He pulled the French press carafe forward, glad he'd snuck out while she was sleeping and bought a couple just-out-of-the-oven scones. It never felt good to be parting on a weekend morning, but the ritual was like religion for Bridget. She felt she had to leave her townhouse in bustling Galway City for the stillness of the countryside. She wanted the quiet to research and think, get ready to "get set," was what she called it. Get set for her battle. He wasn't sure she understood the forces she was up against.

He poured shiny black beans into the grinder, thumbed the power key in spurts and filled the room with the aroma of roast coffee beans. The lid of the electric kettle jiggled just before its lever popped up, and while he waited for the water to come off the boil, he spooned fresh ground coffee into the tempered glass of the French press. Tempered, he thought. That's what I've become, a well-tempered solicitor, plunged from the cold of the business world into the heat of love.

He carried a tray of coffee and warm scones out to the lounge where Bridget sat waiting on the love seat by the window.

"You're spoiling me, Shay. I've not had anyone treat me like this since . . ." She looked away, eyes brimming with unshed tears.

He sat silent for a few moments before he said softly, "Since . . . ?"

"Oh, it's so long ago. Mom would bring out spice cookies hot from the oven every Sunday morning. My favorite." She pursed her lips and blew out a long breath. "Silly of me," she said.

He nodded with a slight frown.

She pulled out a white lace hanky tucked into her sleeve. "My mom's," she said and wiped at her eyes.

He recalled hearing of the car crash in a U.S. nor'easter and ached for her losing her parents like that.

"So long ago," she sighed and put the handkerchief back. "Now," she said, "What do we have here?"

Seamus relaxed and basked in her pleasure over the scones and French roast he had at the ready. Outside, sunlight sparkled on Galway Bay. Sunlight, perfect for this moment, a treasure since rain was sure to be coming soon.

He walked her out to her little red Audi and waved at her departing car, standing there until she turned right off the Long Walk onto Dock Road. He gazed at the empty parking space she'd left in front of her townhouse. Empty. That's how he'd begun to feel when she was not nearby.

It only took him a minute and a half to run around the block to his building and let himself into the nearly empty garage, dark from clouds gathering outside the barred windows. He passed by his sensible Yaris and visualized the Porsche GT2 he would buy after the big money started rolling in.

He moved through the dim space and was startled when old Doc Murphy stepped out of the stairwell. "Morning, Seamus. What you got going so early, dressed in your sport coat and all?"

"Might ask you the same, Doc."

"Had to review dental records, murder case, double check if I'd done the right thing by the detectives. Sad case, that." He coughed and triggered a cascade of hacking.

Seamus waited until the old man recovered himself. "You want to think about getting a partner in with ya, man. I could ask around."

"Going to bring in my granddaughter soon as she finishes dental school over at NUI. Thanks, mate." He tottered off toward his timeworn sedan.

Seamus shook his head. Even if the old dentist wondered at his coming in on a Saturday, it wasn't that odd, given that Seamus's business took up a tenth of the square footage in the building overlooking the docks. It was a mixed use area—town houses bordered the bay inlet where the fisher fleet flourished so long ago while on the back side were commercial yards and offices.

Two at a time, he took the concrete steps up to the landing, and unlocked the steel door to the carpeted hallway. A dozen long strides took him past the dentist's office to his own suite: Hanrahan Solicitors. He was proud to offer a range of legal services including doing real estate work, drawing up wills and setting up businesses.

It had been impossible to turn down Dermot's ambitious proposal back in '09. He'd been so engaging, phoning from Los Angeles and praising the website Seamus had put up to attract overseas investors. Dermot proposed flying over, sounding like an excited country boy as he laid out his vision. And his timing couldn't have been better—the Irish economy was headed straight down the toilet back then, likely to take Seamus's business with it.

"Buy low, sell high," Dermot had crowed. Everything was on the market at bargain prices. He had flown over and spent the weekend with Seamus driving him around County Galway looking for prime land for his dream project, a theme park modeled after Disneyland. His mother was from Galway, Dermot said with a proud grin, before his father dragged her across the sea to Hollywood, chasing crazy notions of becoming a movie star.

It was so different from Seamus's father on the Connemara farm, in their family for generations. Seamus unlocked the office door and walked by Aileen's desk. Monday through Friday, the prim middle-aged woman managed his flourishing website and greeted clients who came by in person. What would she think if she could see the underbelly of his theme park work, and of his getting a percent ownership on opening day? With her Catholic morality, he was certain she would be shocked to the tips of her efficient fingers, her hair would turn stark white. He was lucky to have her. The question of how Bridget would view this shady side of Dermot's project—and his part in it—had to be put aside. Again.

He sat at his desk and gazed out at Galway Bay's murky water. The pale Irish sun was clouded over and on its way west, gathering heat to pour golden on California. He touched the burner cell phone on his desk. Soon the big American would be on EuroBuzz in his Donald Trump intensity.

The plain silver frame on his desk drew his attention. Beautiful Bridget. He traced his thumb over her slightly parted lips. So serious . . . and sensuous. Late last night in her townhouse bed, she lifted her burgundy velvet comforter over his back, pulled it down tight and asked if he wanted to learn to make tacos, American style. He closed his eyes and smiled.

The mobile phone vibrated against his leather desk pad twice before he noticed. He sat back and selected a cigar from the Padron box, rolled it between his fingers and thumb, and lifted it to inhale the musky scent before he set it down. He let the cheap disposable ring four times to show he wasn't a flunky ready to hop to.

"Seamus." Not that he needed to give his name. The phone was only for this project. Easy to take out the battery, break the phone in half and toss it into a public waste bin.

"Drop-dead showdown time," the American barked, always to the point.

"Our lads are still on board," Seamus said, hoping it was true. "They like what you've handed out so far." *What choice did they have, muck poor in the crash. We all sold ourselves to this devil.*

"And the bitch?"

How he talks about Bridget! A flush of shame spread along his cheeks. *And me too much in his pocket to protest.* "Think I've got her near shifting to plan B. Locate it outside the park."

The American let out a quick huff, sounding like dice rolling across a craps table. "This park is for fun and fantasy," he boomed. "I'm not standing for her dragging it down with sorrows from the past."

"Give me a few more days," Seamus hedged. Truth was Bridget had become wedded to getting a memorial built inside the theme park, dedicated to telling the full Irish story.

The developer let out the gravelly yelp that passed for his laugh. "Your bonus money starts up when shovels are in the ground, remember. Better construction shovels than diggers in a graveyard."

Seamus's jaws clenched. "Aye, it'll get done. But it's not going to hurt waiting a bit more if it comes to that."

Silence. Can it be me talking to the man like this? "Ever consider she might have a brilliant idea? Think of what Epcot did for Disney World."

"Pot O'Gold's not for history lessons—it's for pure

fun, what Irish-Americans hold in their hearts about the 'auld sod.' Bridget's out of her fucking mind. It's your job to stop her. Lucky for you, I hate to fire people."

The connection from California to Ireland went dead.

Seamus scowled at the phone in his hand. Diggers in graveyards. He stared at the photo of Bridget. Could he convince her to let it go?

Jaysus.

CHAPTER 3

LODI, CALIFORNIA

GILHOOLEY'S PUB AND GRILL buzzed with a late afternoon crowd. Hillary twirled ice cubes in her high-ball glass and waited for a server to take their dinner orders. She was grateful the place allowed children as long as you sat at a table and not at the bar. Her group occupied themselves with a sampling of starters.

The Irish pub had recently reopened and eating there felt like one more way to shift gears and get ready for the trip. She glanced at Ed, who was focused on the TV nearest their table. Suddenly he raised his Guinness high as San Francisco scored another run. He stood and leaned over to high-five Claire as she screamed, "Go Giants!" She ran up to the TV and bounced a stuffed leprechaun up and down in front of the screen, making orange buttons on his jacket bobble.

Hillary frowned over the antics of her daughter. "Come on, Princess, sit down at the table."

She never knew if she was being a good mother or not to little Claire, who was slight for her age, in the lower range of normal. Claire joined her father last fall as a Notre Dame football fan because she identified with its Fighting Irish leprechaun mascot. When teased by classmates for being shorter than other first graders, she claimed she was one of the little people. Hillary had helped her dress like a leprechaun—a girl one, she insisted, as she also insisted on never letting her strawberry blond hair be cut. Claire was self-conscious about her lack of height, so Hillary fostered her pride in her long thick hair.

Hillary looked out the window, waiting for Roger to join them. She'd asked the waitress to serve him a Guinness when he arrived. He was bringing the fattest check she'd earned as a ghostwriter. The income for her biography on California's Lt. Governor Newsom—hitting the bestseller list already—would add to the pot of money they'd saved.

But it was taxing living under the pressure of Roger's publishing deadlines. Worn out and needing a break, Hillary sipped at the dregs of her whiskey and soda, the tension of the past months on deadline draining away with Jameson's liquid assistance. She loved its slight nutty flavor, its intensity calling for small sips. Her shoulders relaxed their tight hold, and she glanced over to see how Sarah was doing.

The waitress came by to check on them, and Sarah asked for more lemon for her iced tea. Hillary closed her eyes for a moment, wondering if she should order another drink and feeling grateful for Sarah's allergy to alcohol. She could drive them home with no worries.

"Hey, ghostie with the mostie!" Roger sang out, sneaking up behind Hillary and tickling her cheek with a piece of paper as he slid into the fifth chair at the round table. He waved her check in the air. "Ta Dah!"

Hillary laughed and reached for the check, but Roger yanked it away. "Not until you promise to send home stories from Ireland, Dopey."

She hated his nickname for her. He'd kept up their Snow White dwarfs tradition, names foisted on them in their college newspaper days. Their professor dubbed her Dopey and he was called Doc. The name still fit in a way she found ironic. He now doctored facts, putting out an incredibly popular though unauthorized series of tell-all biographies.

"I need a break, Doc, not a working vacation!" Hillary hissed.

"Aw, come on!"

She held out her hand, palm up. "Give it here."

Roger ignored her and turned to Claire, who was bouncing her leprechaun doll up and down.

"Let's go, Giants!" she chanted, basking in the approving grins of some fans nearby. Hillary noticed an old couple sit down at a nearby table and exchange whispers. They frowned, pushed their chairs back and left before anyone came to take their orders.

"Calm down, Princess." Hillary reached out to smooth her daughter's waist-length ponytail. She hated to keep a tight rein on Claire, wanted her to feel loved and approved of, unlike how Hillary had felt as a child.

"Claire." Roger bent and put his face inches from the girl's. "Get your mama to write us a story about ghosts who live in Irish castles. What do you say?"

Claire's green eyes widened and she blinked fast. "Would you, Maaa?"

Hillary sighed. "No. I've had enough writing for a while. We're going to find out about your great grandfather's life back in Galway."

"Please, please! Let's look for green ghosts or old towers, like that!" Claire set her leprechaun down hard on the table's edge, causing it to rock slightly.

"Careful, honey girl," called out Sarah. "This table's none too steady."

"Okay, Gran." Claire bounced her leprechaun in high arcs over her glass of pink lemonade and began singing "Over the Rainbow."

Hillary shook her head. The two of them—the young and the old—would be a challenge on the long trip. Sarah had been like a mother to her and a grandmother to Claire. Hillary turned back to her publisher. "Just give me the check, Doc."

Roger handed it to her. "Keep your eyes and ears open for some kind of story we could work with—maybe like the one you did on their woman president. Or links between the IRA and our valley gangs, something real, not like that 'Sons of Anarchy' on TV." He waggled his thick eyebrows in a kind of Groucho Marx fashion. "Though they do make a pile of dough on that series!"

Roger turned to Ed, who'd been watching their interplay during commercials. "You going for that conference over in Dublin, ya?" Roger nodded at the waitress who set down a glass of foamy stout for him.

"It's supposed to be under wraps." Ed narrowed his eyes, projecting the look of a lean bad cop.

"I heard rumbles." Roger took a long swallow of stout. "Aryan gangs with shamrock tats here in the valley?"

"That's only a possibility. Good to stay ahead of the game. You want a story, go back to her." Ed nodded in his wife's direction. "Ask what her Galway girlfriend's been Skyping her about." Ed turned to assist Sarah as she stood and took a step in the direction of the restroom at the back of the place.

Roger raised his eyebrows and stared at Hillary. She

was watching Sarah walk with care. When Sarah was rehabbing from her hip replacement six months before, she'd fallen. Ever since, Hillary kept a closer eye on her friend, who needed surgery on the other hip, too, but was afraid to go through it again.

As Sarah made her way around the table, Hillary turned back to Roger. "It's nothing," she said, annoyed that Ed would bring up conversations he must have overheard from the other room.

"Nothing?" Roger took hold of a pub menu and glanced at it. "What girlfriend are we talking about?"

Hillary was too tired to resist. She sighed. "Okay, you remember my cousin Ted who died back in '05?"

Roger nodded. Sarah pressed her fingertips on his shoulder as she steadied herself on her circuit around the table. He covered her hand with his own, but kept his eyes fixed on Hillary.

"Well, Teddy was engaged to Bridget Murphy, who was away studying in Ireland when he died. She came over for his memorial service, and we felt a connection right away. She's like a sister I never had." Hillary shot a glance at Claire who'd been begging for a sister of her own, and the old guilt washed over her. She signaled the server for another drink.

"So, what's Ed mean?" Roger asked.

"Well, Bridget's fighting a developer who wants to build some kind of theme park over—"

The table came crashing down, spilling drinks and chicken strip crumbs onto the concrete floor, ice and liquid pooling out in circles. Sarah sat on the floor in the midst of the mess, her glasses askew, and a stunned look on her face.

The owner rushed over. "Are you all right?"

Sarah's face flushed red in contrast to her stark white

hair, falling in two long braids down the front of her shirt. "Forgive me! This hip. Can't trust it!" She started laughing.

The owner turned to a server who was already toweling up the spill. "Get the back room set up. Drinks and onion rings."

Ed leaned down to cup Sarah's elbow while Roger took hold of her other arm. They lifted her to her feet where she stood still a few seconds before she shook them off and brushed at her long denim skirt. "I'm fine. Not even wet!"

Hillary leaned near Sarah and whispered, "Want to go home?"

Sarah shook her head vigorously, her braids dusting the front of her western shirt. She slid her arm into the crook of Ed's elbow. "Come on, Sonny, let's check out that back room, liven it up some!" She clenched her jaw and stepped towards the small banquet room at the rear of the pub.

Roger frowned at Hillary. "Are you sure you want to take her . . ." he muttered, looking in the direction of the vanishing Sarah, "along, so far from home?"

"Can't back out now, would kill her. Pushing seventy but thinks she's never getting old. If she'd get the other hip done, she'd be in much better shape." Hillary flashed a smile she didn't feel. "She'll be okay." Hillary nodded towards her daughter, who was helping wipe the uprighted table. "Would you take Claire back and get her settled? I want to talk to the owner."

Roger swooped up Claire and set her on his shoulder. "Eh, little lady, let's journey on back to the forest, how about it?"

Hillary approached the concerned owner. "I'm sorry about my friend upsetting things. It's her hips—give her trouble at times. I'll be happy to pay for the damages."

"Not a bit of it! I'm not sure about that round table anyway—it's left over from the former owners and our only one like it—time to get rid of it." He placed a "Reserved" sign on the tabletop. "Now, no one will sit there." He grinned. "It looks like you've got a celebration going on. What's the occasion?"

"We're going to Ireland."

"Great! You'll be able to come back and give me the latest in pub happenings."

"We wanted to go there for our honeymoon nearly ten years ago, and it's finally happening."

He nodded in the direction of a short plump woman busy behind the bar. "We've never been, the wife and me."

Hillary promised to check in after the trip. She made her way to the back room, relieved to see its sturdy rectangle of a table. Their drinks had already been replaced along with a couple platters of starters. Sarah had joined the others and they were looking over the dinner menu.

Hillary ordered spinach salad with cranberries and chicken, and a glass of water. She pushed away her fresh whiskey and soda—she would need to drive home after all, considering Sarah's fall. She turned to Roger. He was working on a steaming hot fried onion ring.

"I'm glad you asked back there . . ." she shot a look toward the front of the pub, "asked about Bridget."

Roger nodded and grabbed a napkin to catch crumbs falling off the breaded appetizer.

Hillary picked up a fat golden brown ring. She knew she shouldn't, but reminded herself she was on vacation, never a good time to diet. And it was always easy for her to cast aside thoughts of calories. "I've not had time to run this by you since you kept me glued to the keyboard with that last book." They chewed silently for a few seconds.

"But, about Bridget," Hillary said. "She is Irish-American herself and not too long after that awful winter when Teddy died, her parents were killed." Her salad arrived and she picked up her fork. "Their car slid off the road in a New England storm. Bridget felt a kinship to Ireland and got herself involved in the Galway community. She's been helping them get back on their feet after their economy crashed and burned in '08."

Roger took a long swig of his stout. "So?"

"Okay." Hillary licked her fingers. "Some developer—from California would you believe—made a proposal to build a Disney-type park over there, somewhere in her county. At first, Bridget was in favor, but as time's gone by she's done more research. Now she's pushing for this park to educate the public, alongside its fun and games."

Roger wiped his lips. "Of course, Mr. Developer is not happy over that wrinkle!" He gave a low groan.

Hillary nodded and forked a spinach leaf and pushed it around on her plate. "I know. But she's smart, realistic. Her father was a housing developer on the east coast—so she knows the practical side of business. That's what made my cousin Teddy and her such a good pair, back then."

"Whose theme park is this?" Roger cut his giant hamburger in half, more fastidious with it than with his onion rings, and picked up the thick layers.

Hillary took a drink of water. "I think his name is Dermot. Dermot Connolly? Know him?"

Roger put his burger back down. "Jesus," he muttered. He set his elbows on the table and reached up to rub his fingertips along the edge of his receding hairline. "That guy—thinks he's some kind of West Coast

Donald Trump. Built all sorts of towers and golf courses." He plopped his palms onto the tabletop and stared into Hillary's eyes. "He can be treacherous—not kidding you. In fact, couple years ago I sent out feelers about putting out a biography on him. Soon after, I got a weird package in the mail, a set of leather bull balls—you know those cured scrotums you see for sale in antique western shops?"

Hillary dropped her fork and reached out for her whiskey. "You joking?" Cupping the drink with both hands, she stared over the rim of the glass at Roger as she sipped at the amber fluid. Just a little can't hurt.

"You're a smart cookie yourself," Roger clamped his lips together and shook his head before he carried on, "but I hope you're not thinking of getting mixed up with that dude." He narrowed his eyes and carried on in a firm voice. "He's done worse, too, I can't mention in front of youngsters." His voice rose. "Rumored to run his own version of an Irish Mafia. You might want to talk that over with your friend." Hillary stared at him, her nose wrinkled and lips curled back in shock.

Suddenly the whole table went quiet—Sarah, Ed and Claire were watching them.

"What?" Hillary glanced at the others and picked up her fork. "How's your food?" She fastened a smile onto her face. "Mine looks dang tasty." She took a bite, but it took her some minutes of chewing before she could swallow.

CHAPTER 4

AFTER DINNER Ed headed down the street to his unmarked Chevy Caprice. Hillary reminded Roger she wasn't going to keep her eyes open for stories in Ireland. He laughed. "Fat chance—I know you can't help yourself, Dopey! Stories make themselves up around you!" He took off for his San Francisco condo in his Lexus RC.

Hillary stood next to the curb and watched as Sarah settled her hips slowly into the bucket seat. "How're you feeling?" asked Hillary.

"Never better!" Sarah smiled and waggled her shoulders. "Could use a hand with this seat belt, though." Hillary pulled down the strap and bent forward to push the buckle into its metal pocket. She cringed as Sarah winced. *That fall. Have to watch her more closely.*

Claire had fastened herself into her booster, seatbelt wrapped around the leprechaun as well. Hillary started up her car, grateful the old VW Golf still ran well. She would need a new car when Claire got bigger. Hillary's own mother had been petite in contrast to her chubby daughter. Before Claire was born, Hillary used to feel envious, almost hostile, toward what she thought of as the "little people."

Now, it was different. Now she had her own elfin daughter. And old as Ed and she were now, he still wanted more. How would he feel if he knew she'd been taking the pill? Until lately. She shook her head and turned up the volume on the local country music station, one of her favorite ways to cover up troublesome thoughts.

At home, Ed was waiting near the back porch. Hillary no sooner turned off the ignition than Claire jumped out and ran to her father. Ed opened the door and patted her on the bottom as she skipped in. She turned and wiggled her leprechaun against his belly, making him bend over laughing before she darted into the house.

Hillary smiled. What an odd mixture of silliness and smarts she was. Claire—a good name for her, from the Latin meaning clear, bright, shining. Hillary knew she herself had been a somber child, not much fun for her artistic mother. Hillary recalled the peacock-patterned silk scarf her mother tied around her shoulders that first day of second grade. The minute her mother drove away, Hillary had whipped it off and stuffed it into her pocket, flushed with embarrassment over the flashy apparel.

She sighed, got out and walked around to stand by Sarah who placed one foot at a time on the clay hardpan, held on to the doorframe and stood straight up to face Hillary as Ed joined them.

"Okay, you two!" Sarah waved them aside. "I'm fine—don't need any escort. Not unless you've got a good-looking single man hidden in your pocket." She laughed.

"Thanks for dinner!" She tottered off to her mother-in-law cottage.

They waited until she got inside and turned on her lights.

Hillary pushed the remote to lock her car. "Think she'll be okay?"

"She's got those Miwok genes," Ed said. "They've kept her strong all these years. It would kill her if we didn't take her along, now." Ed slipped his arm around Hillary's waist. "Come on, rich writer woman, let's get you to bed—you deserve some time off." He nuzzled her hair.

While Ed and Claire brushed their teeth, Hillary rifled through papers she'd slipped into her suitcase. She'd drawn her version of the family tree, rooted on the stony shore of the River Corrib, and highlighted connections among relatives. Last on her chart was Claire. Hillary loved her child, but sometimes Claire went well beyond challenging. Probably she thought she was just being playful, but if you gave her lined paper, she could be counted on to write perpendicular to the lines. And laugh at your amazement.

Hillary's thoughts stretched back among the worn grooves of the past, reaching to remember what she herself was like before she was ten. How much trouble had she been? What could she have done to make her mother run off? She could almost hear herself complaining when she was made to stand perfectly still on that old footstool and turn around a few inches at a time while her mother marked hemlines with straight pins for skirts and dresses. "Why can't I just get clothes from the store?" Hillary would whine. Okay, she was also a nosy kid. Looked through her mother's dresser drawers. Her nightstand. What had she found? Nothing came to mind. A darkness suffused her memories, palpable as a brick wall painted black.

Hillary sighed and slipped the family tree behind the other papers inside the lid of her suitcase, mindlessly shoving aside an old rosary she'd taken along on trips before. She'd have to go over Claire's packing tomorrow, couldn't let it slide. Like her mother had let everything go.

She would never abandon Claire, no matter if lately she got flashes of understanding what could have driven her mother away. How could she trust herself? What if something came over her when Claire reached the age of ten? Only three more years to go. Would the sins of the mother be visited on the second and third generations?

Maybe she should try to find her mother, see if she could figure out what triggered her to run off like that. Any mention of her had been rebuffed by Hillary's father. They both buried their feelings. She grew up following in his footsteps and became a reporter, focused on the facts of the news, the cool undisturbing facts. Father and daughter. So much alike. If only he were still alive, she had the courage to press him on it now. Too late.

Time to say goodnight. Claire had already gotten herself into a nightgown and tucked into bed, waiting for her father's bedtime story. Sometimes Ed seemed like a mother to Claire. It bothered Hillary but she didn't know what to do about it. She bent to kiss Claire on the top of her blond head but before she could, her daughter jumped out of bed. "Night, Maaa!" She ran down the hall and returned in a flash, dragging her laughing father by the hand.

Hillary stood at the bathroom mirror, struggling to overcome feeling abandoned by her daughter, and began removing her makeup. She thought back to the days when she didn't need any, just ran around with her face fresh and natural.

At forty-four, wrinkles were making themselves known at the corners of her eyes and tiny vertical lines shot up from her lips. Her freckles had become more pronounced over the years since she'd married Ed and moved away from her cottage in cool dark Morada to this sunny farmhouse.

She rubbed a face wipe lightly across her eyelids, sighed and blinked her eyes as an eyelash pricked against her lid. Peering close to the mirror, she looked for the errant lash. Jeez, bags under my eyes. Got to get a good night's sleep. She blinked fast to tear up and nudge the dark copper lash over to where she could edge it out with her fingertip.

Ed walked in and stood behind her. "Are you crying?"

"Just an eyelash. Do you think I look old? Be honest."

"If you looked any younger, I might get picked up for statutory." He smiled. "Come on, Claire let down Rapunzel's long hair again, and she's nodded off. Now it's time to put my hardworking redhead to bed."

She relaxed, her heart lifted by this man she knew she could trust with anything. Almost.

"Ummm," he murmured and ran his palms lightly alongside her arms. She tossed her face-wipe into the wastebasket and leaned her head back against his cheek.

"You're gorgeous, Chickadee." He'd started calling her that way back when. She still didn't fully get what it meant, but his tones of love and lust put it beyond the need to know.

He stroked her belly. "Don't need anything on your skin—I love your dimpled face."

She shut her eyes and rolled her shoulders against his chest. He turned her around, lifted her chin and planted a long kiss on her naked lips.

Claire burst into the bathroom, waving her Rapunzel doll in one hand and with her other pulling at her own hair and wailing, "It's not getting longer."

"I thought you were sleeping," Hillary said.

"I was just pretending. I can't sleep."

"Did you try?" Hillary asked.

Ed smiled at their daughter, dressed in a princess nightgown, barefooted and pulling at the foot-length hair of her doll.

"You both look perfect to me," Ed said.

"Punzy's hair is long as she is," Claire said, and yanked at her own hair, reaching to her waist.

"Yours is still growing," Hillary said. "It takes time. When you were born, you didn't have any at all."

"If I ever have a baby sister, she better be bald." Claire stamped her foot and pursed her lips.

Ed laughed and walked his daughter back to her room.

Hillary smoothed night cream over her face. She welcomed its tingle—the security of keeping her nakedness covered even if lightly—and waited for her husband to come back.

"When are we going to make a sister or brother for Claire?" He rubbed up against Hillary's back. "Hmm? We've got plenty of money now for baby number two."

Not that again. She had no answer. Not one she could share.

"Nothing to stop us," she murmured and turned to face him, belly to belly.

Ed was pushing her—and she liked it. He had changed since he'd finally tracked down the hit and run bastard who'd killed his teenaged daughter from his first marriage. His trust in his detective powers was back—stronger than ever. He lifted her chin and dusted her open lips with tiny kisses.

"Do it, daddy man," she moaned.

She reached over and snapped off the light. The moonlight shining through the windows was enough. They laughed in unison, low and deep. Sometimes Ed's romantic attentions sent her into a dreamless sleep and she yearned for some tonight.

Her mother was leaving, no suitcase at all—just the tiny woman, paintbrushes in one hand, artist's pallet in the other. Morphed into a flat slip of a figure, weaving in and out among dolls and stuffed animals piled into corners, her mother slid out through a crack at the top of the locked bedroom window. When she woke and ran to her parents' room, it was true. She was not good enough for her mother to stay. Not good enough.

Hillary woke on the edge of a sob, her nightgown clammy against her skin. In the middle of changing to a dry gown, the image of Sarah on the floor at Gilhooley's hit her between the eyes.

Forget the past. On this trip she would focus on being a good mother to Claire and like a good daughter to Sarah, as well. Could she keep them both safe?

Ed's gentle snores interrupted her worries. What a great partner he was. She had to relax for this break—he would be at her side when she needed him.

CHAPTER 5

SEAMUS LOCKED HIS OFFICE DOOR even though it wasn't necessary. He had the urge to hide this side of himself, grown over the years since he started dealing with Dermot. Got to get to it. He bent and unlocked a bottom file drawer and pulled out a couple of manila folders. It was time to phone around, remind his guys on the planning committee about the right way to vote. Again. And remind them why—the two were still on the young side and poor, eager to accept Dermot's financial backing for their startup businesses. The way he'd been back then.

He sighed, opened a cabinet and took out a cylinder of rolled blueprints. It never hurt to review selling points before he called. The benefits that would come for his guys' new ventures as part and parcel of Dermot's project. Seamus couldn't imagine what he would do if one of them backed out now.

He spread out the design plans, anchored them with beanbags at the four corners and put on his reading glasses. His fingers traced the features of Dermot's Pot

39

O'Gold. "Battles by the Boggy Waters" with its underground journey through ancient ritual sacrifices could easily rival "Pirates of the Caribbean." Then there was the skull-shaking "Skeleton Bones" roller coaster plunging a hundred feet underground for the thrill seekers and the gentle "Over the Rainbow" ride for the little ones. Yes, the park had been a splendid idea. Get millions of descendants of Irish emigrants to come visit the Ireland of their dreams, the one they knew through Americanized songs and movies.

With a handkerchief pulled from his pants pocket, he wiped his sweaty brow and then his palms. He retrieved the burner phone from the bottom file drawer, the one for his guys, and punched in a number. Letting it go to voice mail, he left his usual message to call back. Then he did the same for the other guy. They needed time to get away someplace private to return his calls.

He began putting away the blueprints and was startled to hear the buzzing vibration of a callback so quickly.

"Yeah," he answered, in the terse fashion he'd taken up during his years associating with Dermot.

"What's up?" It was John Murphy, a butcher from Gort who wanted to start up a superstore down south county way. Seamus had kept John's loyalty with broad hints of the added opportunity to also open a small retail outlet inside the park once it became a reality.

"Just reminding you of the vote coming up. And Dermot's ready to transfer funds into your account."

"Gotcha. But I'm fearin' that woman getting in the papers lately. She might win over the others with her whacky ideas about displayin' our sorrows, give 'em respect. I might have to go along with her, for decency, ya' ken what I mean?" He cleared his throat.

Seamus could feel his pulse race. "If we stick together, we can shift her proposal outside the park somewhere, you know? It's not that upbeat for vacationers comin' for a good time."

"You're likely right. I don't want to focus on the past—ride the wind of the future, is my belief." John laughed. "But still . . ."

"Don't give in to doubt, man. We can all ride the new prosperity wave. I'll speak to you soon." Seamus disconnected.

What would Dermot do if one or God forbid both councilmen switched his vote to deny Bridget's memorial inside the theme park? Dermot wanted to build on 95 acres up near Tuam he'd bought after he couldn't get his hands on acreage in Coole Park. The park was an idea for its time, all right—promote tourism and catch the surge of upward economic momentum after the long recession, revive the economic beast they'd nicknamed the Celtic Tiger.

He patted his breast pocket, tempted to light up a Padron. His office was one of the places a man could still smoke after the indoor pub ban ten years ago. Another do-gooder success.

But it was too early for a cigar. Nicaraguan cigars. One of the perks he could afford now. He reflected on the boggy road he'd travelled over the last five years, working on this project, sinking down by stages—first out in the light, then negotiating in secret, then on to what some could consider bribery. Dermot's intentions were good, though. Seamus sighed and rubbed the stubble of his cheeks. One thumb played with the bristly dimple in his chin while with the other hand, he picked up the framed photo of Bridget and stared at her serious expression.

Dermot had introduced him to Bridget. She started out as a consultant from the economic growth team, in favor of the theme park proposal to bring in more tourists. But over the last year, her opposition to a park stuffed with stereotypes of the Irish had become a massive problem. Now, she headed a small group of idealists with too much time on their hands, insisting Dermot construct a memorial to honor Irish sufferings as a condition of permitting him to build glittering amusements in a fantasy Ireland.

At first, Dermot wanted Seamus to handle Bridget the same as the guys on the planning council. With her, though, even the suggestion of bribes had been pointless, independently wealthy as she was. Friendly persuasion had been a better tactic to try on this woman. And he'd been working on her in a playful way, enjoying his growing skills at pillow talk. Last night had been perfect. He grew hot around the collar remembering what happened after he caressed her all over with butterfly kisses.

Later, he brought up her memorial and suggested a vacant building right in the middle of the tourist section near Galway Bay.

"That would bring folks in at a time when they're more open to the history," he said.

"It needs to be in the park where visitors can feel the full sweep of our agonies along with our mysteries and joys," she replied. "Like we are learning about each other's." She had grinned, rolled over and dozed off. He feared that woman wasn't made for backing down.

Seamus sighed and ran his fingers through his thick curls several times before he checked his watch. He hadn't heard back from his other guy, Brian. He stared out the window at Dock Road, seeing nothing. Damn. He wished he'd thought this project through more before he got in so deep. And had known that damn Dermot better.

Suddenly the phone buzzed, yanking him out of his reverie. It was Brian, who hissed he couldn't talk on the phone but needed to meet in person down at Garvey's.

Seamus put away the folders and blueprints and closed up the office. He made his way toward Shop Street, threading through tourists packing the pedestrian thoroughfares. Business was coming back after the long recession. And more than just fiddlers with their hats set out on the street to garner coins for their entertainment. A troupe of four actors garbed in whiteface twirled silk scarves in all colors and called out breathy hoots to beckon a crowd around them. Seamus breathed in deep, his chest swelled with joy. Their Celtic Tiger was about to start roaring again in the theme park. But it wouldn't be worth getting a bite taken out of his Bridget.

He walked into Garvey's public bar and spotted Brian at a table, but suddenly his Dermot-only phone vibrated in his pocket. He couldn't take a call from the big shot in front of Brian, didn't want to look like a damn puppet. He darted back to the men's toilet, glad to see he was alone, and slipped into one of the two stalls. Had to hurry. The men's room in a pub was a popular place.

"Yeah," he muttered into the cheap burner.

"You're failing," Dermot barked. "Just heard she plans an announcement next week. New findings supporting her crazy ideas. We're not in the clear. You're not persuasive enough with that broad."

Seamus felt his heart pounding against his ribs.

"She's strong willed. It's a shaky tripod I'm on—romance, business, politics." Dermot should know that, the bastard. Been married three times, for feck's sake.

Seamus could hear the bathroom door squeak open.

"Heard she plans a bombshell to fire at the next planning meeting. Why didn't you clue me she's charging us with cannibalizing the local attractions?"

"What do you mean?" Seamus whispered. He could hear someone unzipping, getting busy at the urinal.

"Think I'd be stupid enough to have just one Irisher on my team? Your lust for her is blinding you. I can only give you a couple more days," Dermot growled. He cleared his throat. "She needs to drop her hot potato and keep it dropped. Or I'll send in a stronger motivator."

"Why in such a hurry now?" The man at the urinal sounded like a horse pissing—no need to worry about his overhearing the conversation. "Good things take time here."

"Doctors are giving Ma," Dermot sucked in a noisy breath, "dammit, a year or two at most. You know what it means to get her back to Ireland, see what I've built in her name. Waited too long already. It's time to get those shovels biting up dirt."

Click.

Shovels in the ground. Again. Seamus flushed the toilet to make it seem like a normal visit to the stall in case someone was listening. Stronger motivator. What did that mean?

Bridget. He slapped his hand against his chest to quiet the pounding inside. In a daze, he washed his hands at the sink.

"Hey, mate, jolly good game—Cork versus Galway." The American who'd had plenty of Guinness blabbed on in what he must have thought was an Irish accent.

Irish Americans, thought Seamus. Full of sentimental nonsense and Dermot poised to take their money to indulge their fantasies. He splashed water on his face and stood unfocused at the mirror, envisioning the specter of what Dermot might have in store for Bridget. But who would he get, to do what? Dermot himself wouldn't soil his hands from construction shovels in the ground or any other kind of dirty work. Besides, he was an ocean away in California. Not that his location ever stopped him from getting what he wanted. Seamus shook his head, squared his shoulders and went to find his guy drumming his fingernails on the pub tabletop.

"I'm in a hurry, mate," Brian said. "My old lady's taken up her brother's cause—he's got a little furniture shop downtown, nearly going broke. Now she's supporting All-Irish business and complaining about politicians on the take from developers." He downed the last of his stout and wiped his mouth with the back of his hand. "I couldn't discuss this on the phone, ya know."

Seamus nodded sympathetically as Brian rambled on. "Made an excuse 'bout needin' to get out of the house for work, but thinkin' I might not be able to come through for you."

Seamus explained the vote might be put off anyway. There could be some kind of news that tabled the proposal. Brian said he was getting worn out battling a father and son in Coole Park who were on the All-Irish committee fighting to keep the region small and quaint like in the old days. They didn't want any big theme park or hotels—thought the B&Bs and the Lady Gregory Hotel was plenty in the area. But Brian himself was still trying to be on board—wanted the chance to get his new hotel project started after the theme park got rolling.

He's on the money train like me, Seamus thought and then told Brian to wait for further direction.

Seamus strode back to his office building and jumped into his car. He sped through Galway. What could he say to convince Bridget to drop her demands? Talk her committee into sensible development? He'd taken up with her as part of the business deal with Dermot, but the pert and savvy business consultant had changed direction over the past year at the same time she'd captured his heart.

His heart. He thought he'd kept it walled away until he had made his fortune as the second son, not going to inherit the farm in Connemara. Bridget's proposal to the planning council was outrageous, actually. Why would a theme park want to dim its sparkling fantasyland with a Memorial Museum? Sadden everyone up. She had to back off her idealistic posture, but he couldn't reveal Dermot's threats. There must be a way to get through to her.

CHAPTER 6

COUNTRY HOUSE OUTSIDE GALWAY, IRELAND

SEAMUS DROVE PAST the clots of tourists bulging out beyond the pedestrian-only streets, watching for their unpredictable reactions to the street-theater performers. He barely missed a couple boys darting in front of him, followed by a short blond toddler. Where in hell are the parents?

His arms hung heavy on the steering wheel, leaden with fear over Dermot's words. Bridget was too much in the public eye to harm, wasn't she?

Their agreement was she had weekends to herself out at her country house, her phone off. Last night was one of the evenings she set aside to play. She was so disciplined. How would she would take his bursting in on her?

He clenched his jaw to steady his nerves as he crept along the street. Traffic was heavy past Eyre Park, and the music everywhere annoyed him today. New Orleans jazz blasted out from a trombone, trumpet and drums while a set of redheaded twins in harlequin sang their lungs out. A light rain had passed and the air was dense with moisture. Nothing was as certain in Ireland as the weather changing—now he had to get Bridget to change.

His car at a standstill, he cleared his throat and cracked open the door to spit into the street but his mouth was too dry. He glanced up and marveled at clouds rolling along in the sky like fluffy marshmallows. He knew he had to convince her to shift her momentum on this thing.

He got clear of the crush of tour buses and onto the bridge over the River Corrib. The fishermen whipping their flies back and forth into the rocky waters calmed him a bit. Some things never change, since long ago when the Claddagh village king ruled here. This was the real Ireland, not the fantasy Dermot wanted to construct. His fingers tightened on the steering wheel.

But it was complicated. Pot O'Gold would bring jobs and more tourist money. Seamus sighed as he drove by Galway Business Park where he'd guest lectured for the Cairnes School. His heart softened and face warmed despite the cool breeze. He recalled the moment when he met Bridget, a smart and sexy post-doctoral student in Irish history hired by Dermot to consult on authenticity for his theme park plans. Dermot wanted to attract Americans of Irish ancestry. He planned to include free genealogical research banks, rides named after fairies and folk characters, and to mingle all that with sayings like, "You're not really drunk if you still have a blade of grass to hang on to" and "Luck of the Irish."

She knows how to dig up more history than is good for her, he mused. Digging. Shovels in the ground, was how Dermot put it. Visions of men harvesting peat bogs, slicing slabs of heavy soil, flashed through his mind. The sacrifice of ancient Irish kings into boggy waters was one of the attractions Dermot planned to feature in Pot O'Gold.

Seamus shuddered at the thought of sacrifice. And how brave a crusader his Bridget had become.

He drove past front gardens chock full of fuchsias, hydrangeas and begonias, past rock walls set behind rows of pine trees and got onto the N59. Thank Jaysus, Bridget didn't live far out on the poorly maintained road. It was hell the way the tourist buses and lorries beat up the surface—bumpy as a devil's road.

Years ago when he first showed Dermot around, searching for a good location for the park, they took the N59 up the Connemara coast to Clifden. Dermot had studied maps and thought somewhere up there would be good. But after the trip they agreed it was a foul idea. Tourists wouldn't swarm by the thousands to a place demanding so rough a ride to get to.

Seamus pulled into Bridget's driveway, lined with roses of red, orange and white. He parked behind her car and walked back to the roadside to pick up her Sunday *Irish Times*, surprised at how unwieldy the bundle of newsprint was, lacking a rubber band around the thick wad of pages. He was startled to find a little figure a few inches from where he had picked up the *Times*. It looked like a doll made from a bit of white cloth, its head above a neck made from a rubber band.

What the blasted devil?

He pocketed the cloth figure and shoved the *Times* under his arm. He knocked on her front door and waggled the knob. Locked.

Good. He waited, glad he didn't have to use the key she'd given him a few months back. She'd said it was just in case. In case of what, he wondered.

Suddenly, there she was, dragging her fingers through her long black hair, her green eyes wide, as if coming out of a horror film at a local theater.

"Shay!" She stepped aside to let him in. "What are you doing here?"

"Special delivery, milady." He handed her the *Times*. "Truth is I couldn't stay away, after last night." He reached out and cradled her face in his hands. The heavy Sunday newspaper fell to the floor, unnoticed. He could feel her pulse racing against his palms. They stood pressed belly to belly, lips locked as moments passed.

But then she took a step back and gazed up at him. With a quick snap, she shook her head. "I've been finding out more." She pointed toward the highway. "It's definite my own road was lined with the starving, stumbling along trying to get to the city and something to eat, falling into roadside ditches in the freezing air of eighteen forty-seven. And I drive right over it all the time without a thought for what they suffered."

A tear rolled down her cheek. She brushed at it and walked through the lounge into her office to point to her desk, piled with stacks of books. A couple of old volumes sat open, held by what looked like beanbags on the corners. "I've just come to the places where the worst is described. It's beyond belief," she whispered. She stared at Seamus. He shook his head in silence. "And last week when I was planting new roses," she nodded toward her garden, "I came across . . . ." She fell silent, staring into his eyes.

"What? What did you come across?" His heart pounded in his chest.

"Never mind, it's being looked into now." She shook her head and took a firmer tone: "But Dermot has a chance to show the world we respect and grieve for what the poor went through." She picked up the *Times*, walked into her lounge and waved the fat bundle of newspaper at a framed verse hanging above her mantel. "They had it immensely worse than I ever did when they died," she gestured at the framed photos of Teddy and her parents sitting on her mantel, "and left me an orphan over here." She read aloud the calligraphied words on her wall.

> Turn to me and have pity on me
> For I am alone and in misery
> —Psalm 25:16

"Think of their souls in misery, alone as their loved ones faded away, and still, today decomposing into the soil, never laid properly to rest. I don't dare go digging out there in the ditches beyond the roses—no one else does either. We're a nation haunted by their ghosts." She sank onto a velour sofa, her shoulders sagging.

Seamus sat next to her, feeling overwhelmed. He'd never seen her like this and was unsure if he should show her the rag doll he'd found near her newspaper. "There *are* some memorials, you know," he said, watching for her reaction, " . . . the Docks famine sculpture in Dublin and even here the standing stone at Salthill on the beach, in memory of that little girl." He reached for Bridget's hand.

She yanked her hand away and stood. "But, there are hundreds and thousands more who lived and died without mention—I feel for them, and I wasn't even born here!" She paced in circles. "A better memorial can be built, and without harming the theme park. I know it can!"

She pointed to a framed calligraphy on the opposite wall, this in a Celtic design, and read it aloud, as if Seamus wouldn't understand otherwise.

> People will not look forward to posterity
> Who never look backward to their ances-
> tors.
> —Edmund Burke

Her eyes took on a horror-movie look again. "We've got to show the whole story and in a place where no one will be able to keep it hushed up."

Seamus cleared his throat. "But, Bridge, think about it. How many theme parks anywhere have something negative, something depressing in their attractions?" He didn't want to bring up Disney's educational theme park exploring various cultures—he hadn't been to Epcot, but he knew it was not all fun and games.

Bridget scowled. "In California, Shay, they have a state park with a museum in memory of the Donner Party, those pioneers who got snowbound crossing the Sierras. All I'm asking is a way to honor our fallen, show how far they had to go to try and survive. It's not so much, is it?"

He pulled the ghostly doll figure out of his pocket and dangled it in front of her. "But you're getting warned to keep off this path you're stuck on following. Can't you let it drop, or at least retouch it in positive terms—the heroics of some folks who struggled to make the best of a bad situation." He felt like falling on his knees to beg her to stop.

She began laughing until she was choking, doubled over with howls that ran on for long seconds. Seamus felt like a fool, his cheeks hot with his mix of dread and passion for this crusader woman, so odd a love for a practical man like himself.

"Oh," she wiped at her cheeks streaked with tears of laughter mixed with her earlier sorrow. "Oh, you darling!" She smiled. "I can't let those tiny rags scare me away. This project is bigger than that. Can't you see?"

"Those tiny rags? There've been more?"

"A few," she said.

He took both her hands in his. "The developer is much more powerful and determined than you may have realized," he said.

"Poo on him—call him by his name: Dermot. I don't believe there is anything he can do to hurt me. What I want is not harmful for him! Not if he gets on board with it now."

"Now?"

"I've learned some things he'd want to keep buried in the past."

Seamus didn't want to uncover Dermot's secrets. "At least move your idea outside the park."

"It wouldn't get overlooked in there, the way so many of our memorials have. The park is a perfect place to balance showing our wonder and our woe."

Seamus searched his brain for what to say to turn her in a new direction. The lines from the Wizard of Oz scarecrow flew into his mind. A brain. He didn't get a brain. He got a paper diploma. Paper.

"Excuse me. I need to use . . . ." He left the lounge and shut the bathroom door.

He pulled a cigar from his breast pocket and wiggled the paper band. It was stuck firmly to the outside leaf of the cigar as usual. Normally he left it on until the thing was half smoked and warm from that. He turned on the hot water in Bridget's sink and held the stogie under the running water until the tobacco leaf softened and the band gave way and slipped off into his fingers. With care he dried both items and stuck the cigar back into his breast pocket then slipped the band onto his little finger. It was perfect, a cream-colored band bordering a central oval stamped with Padron and supported by tiny gold leaves below. Padron meant quality.

Really not all that bad for the time being. Could even have it encased in clear acrylic later, for sentimental reasons.

He went to find Bridget. She was seated at her desk and bent forward over an old book, holding the pages open. He knelt down on one knee next to her side.

"What if we get married and have a couple little ones to carry on for us. You wouldn't want to put them in danger, now would you?" It didn't feel so odd, here in the marriage proposal posture. "You can teach them all you know and have them carry the stories into the future. Marry me, Bridget."

She flung herself back against her chair, hands waving in the air like angel wings, the book snapping shut. "Now you are scaring me, Mr. Confirmed Irish Bachelor."

"It's what we both want, but haven't said, isn't it?" Seamus felt a tightness in the back of his throat. "You know it's gone beyond how we started out in the business park." He lifted his pinkie and took off the band. He rubbed his other palm lightly over the top of it. "Abracadabra, let this band stand in for a Claddagh ring." He held it out to her. "Will you be my bride?"

Her jaw fell open.

She pushed back her chair, stood and heaved a deep sigh. "I want this, too. But not this way. Not out of fright. Go. Get out. We have to push on for the memorial, for better or for worse." She strode to the front door, and flung it open. "Go!" She stood stony faced while Seamus slowly got off his knee, and went to her.

"You are making a mistake, my love," he whispered and kissed her on both cheeks. She stood rigid at the open door, as a cold wind blew in.

He turned and walked to his car, feeling a lump of fear in his throat that he could neither swallow nor spit out.

CHAPTER 7

LODI VINEYARD, CALIFORNIA

HILLARY WAVED at Ed's unmarked car as he drove away, parallel to the rows of grapes. San Joaquin County Sheriff's Department was lucky to have him. He was going in on a Sunday to tie up loose ends and finish preparation for terrorist training for the new position he'd start when they got back. She fed the yellow labs, Daisy and her puppy Rufus, who gobbled up their breakfast and dashed away into the fields.

The dry heat of the Central Valley set a languid tone humming through her bones. She glanced at the bright blue sky. If only it were always daylight, if dark never fell, bringing murky dreams. Tomorrow they would be up in that sky, flying.

This morning was her last chance to Skype with Bridget. It was late afternoon in Ireland and here, Claire and Sarah were not yet up and about, needing her. The treasure of a quiet morning. She smiled.

Lying front and center on the oak desk in her office was her trusty MacBook Air, her main tool for Roger's assignments. He'd expanded his weekly newspaper into a successful enterprise publishing biographies of celebrities. He'd had to take Hillary off her job as a bylined reporter for *The Acorn*. A couple articles she'd written in college had been cited in a study of plagiarism and gone viral on the internet. Hillary's face burned with shame every time she thought of it. Roger hadn't any choice, really, and neither had the chair at the college where she'd lost her position as student paper faculty advisor.

She should have been able to stop herself, but that compulsion had come over her. It was those stories about bad mothers that threw her over the top and out of her mind. They turned her into someone she didn't recognize and draped over her shoulders what she called her "P" problem. She'd lost her Hillary Broome byline. Her father would be so humiliated at what she'd done to his name.

She sighed, slumped into her chair and clicked the Skype icon. Bridget answered right away, her bright face cheering up Hillary.

"Want to be a matron of honor?" Bridget sang out. She laughed, looking younger than Hillary'd seen her in months. "We could make it a vacation plus wedding trip."

"You've got Seamus ready to commit?" Hillary wondered if this man was good enough for her friend.

"You've heard of the Irish male—waits for middle age before marriage. He's worried about me now though, his cave-man instincts are in high gear."

"What happened?"

"He panicked over this little guy." Bridget dangled a tiny white ragdoll in the Skype window, snapped its rubber-banded neck and jiggled it to make its fabric corners dance.

"Holy Mary. Looks like a handkerchief skirt. Where did that come from?"

"This little lad was alongside my *Irish Times* yesterday morning. Last week, it was a bigger one, from the *Times* plastic wrapper on a rainy morning. I asked my delivery man about it, but he swears he knows nothing." She squinched up her face. "Think someone wants to scare me off?"

"Ha. Fat chance." Hillary ignored the slim needle of fear pricking her throat. "Maybe a message to keep your nose clean, but they don't know you. Seamus thinks marriage will stop the ghost doll parade?"

"Maybe, but . . ."

"What?"

"I didn't say 'yes.' In fact I sent him packing. Marriage and a family will bank my fire to get the museum into the park. But we're close to winning council approval, so next week, I'll give him a different answer." She winked. "He had a cigar band ready to slip on my finger." She laughed. "Pretty passionate and impulsive, ya?"

"Hmmm. Not sure that's a good sign." This man sounded none too stable, not like her Ed who could be counted on.

Bridget changed the subject. "Speaking of marriage and family, I might get some new Broome secrets soon."

Hillary beamed with joy. "I'm bringing along Dad's papers." She took a swig of coffee, cooled off the way she liked it. "And a family tree I've drawn. I can't wait to fill in gaps in the story. Like why Fianna left California to go back to Ireland. Made Grandad so mad he tried to cut women out of the business." It was horrible what he had done to the family, pushed them to the brink of murder.

Bridget frowned. "Fianna's son is giving me an old trunk full of his mother's things. He said there are stories certain people would kill to keep private."

"Fianna's life puts you in danger?"

"Not sure, but other bits I've found deep in the internet," she reached out and patted the face of her computer, "this big old desktop is still laboring away for me," she smiled. "Some academic papers I've dug up are bombshells." She shook her head, frowning. "I might toss one or two of them into council planner laps at the meeting next month. Get 'em to see why we need more than just fun and games." Bridget sucked in a deep breath and blew it out, her lips forming a bee-stung bow.

"You be careful, you!" Hillary said, shaking her head. "Are you still taking those midnight walks?"

"Calms me down. After a day of research I like to go into town and walk along the bay in the cool night. I keep a sharp eye out. Carry pepper spray, too."

"Make sure you do." Hillary felt worried and excited at the same time. Good thing she'd kept up karate at the Lodi dojo. Her training had come in handy before, but that was nearly ten years ago. "And, yes, I'll stand up with you if you go through with a wedding."

"Wedding, what wedding?" Claire burst into the office, startling Hillary. "Hi, Auntie Bridget!" Claire pushed her face front and center so she showed up like a giant on the Skype screen.

"You can be my flower girl, aye?" Bridget beamed.

"With four-leaf clovers in my hair!" screamed Claire, stretching out a hank of her blond hair.

Bridget laughed. "Most of ours have just three leaves, but we can look for the lucky ones. Have your mom braid them into our hair." She lifted strands of her black hair.

Claire nodded. "The three of us—blond, black, and redhead!" She stroked her mother's face. "And Grannie Sarah—white! Four colors." She shrieked with laughter.

Hillary nodded, her caffeine level felt doubled by the energy of her daughter.

"Can't wait to welcome you all!" cried Bridget. "Failte! That's Irish for welcome." She spelled out the word. "But, we say it 'fall-cha.' "

Hillary and Claire repeated after her a few times.

Bridget nodded. "Right! You've got it!"

Hillary disconnected, feeling the warmth of friendship. What a wonderful invention, Skype.

"Maaa, I want pancakes," Claire wailed as she smoothed her doll's long blond hair. "So does Punzy."

Hillary set her cast iron griddle on the stove. It was already so hot raising the mercury a bit more would hardly make a difference. She mixed pancake batter from scratch and ladled some into a Mickey Mouse shape—Claire's favorite ever since they'd gone to Disneyland last year.

Afterward, they went outside and checked on some of the grapes, plump and nearing their peak. The earthy smells from the warm soil and the dusty grapes soothed Hillary's nerves and made her feel like a cat purring in the sunlight. Heavy bunches hung with the promise of a rich harvest. Zinfandel was what they specialized in, as well as a bit of the old vine Tokay the region started with so long ago, with its promise of mirroring the bounty of the sunny Mediterranean soil. Hillary and Ed had lucked into being part of a group Roger put together when the acreage west of Lodi came on the market.

Hillary sat on a hammock and patted her lap. Claire

placed a milking stool between her knees. Hillary drew a brush over and through her daughter's long hair, soothed by the repetitive motion. Hillary tried to picture her mother brushing her hair. Or taking time for anything Hillary wanted, anything to make her feel good, but she couldn't remember a thing.

"Maaa, will we get to see leprechauns?" Claire's question broke into Hillary's daydream. Hillary liked the way Claire had taken to calling her "Maaa," pulling the word out long, like a little lamb bleating.

"No, sweets. Those are not real. Just for fun in Irish stories."

"How about four leaf clovers? For Auntie Bridget's bouquet."

Bouquet. It was amazing how much a young girl knew about weddings. Was it in the female DNA? "Well, we can look for Irish shamrocks over there. See if they have any with four leaves. Think they're in the same family."

Hillary braided her daughter's thick hair into one fat plait down the middle of her back, reaching past her waist. "Have to find out more about the luck of the Irish."

Claire's hair had been left uncut since she was three years old and heard the story of Rapunzel. In nearly four years, her thick locks had grown to hip length and would have been impossible to brush through without detangling spray. Never a whimper escaped her mouth except when anyone suggested how much cooler it would be with short hair in the hot Central Valley summers. A couple times, Sarah mentioned how wonderful it would be to donate her beautiful hair for wigs for little children bald from cancer treatments. But Claire balked at any such thoughts.

61

Now Hillary fastened her daughter's braid with a pink satin ribbon tie. "Okay, off you go."

Claire picked up her wooden stool and ran to the back porch. Daisy and Rufus bounded alongside her. She set the stool in the corner of the porch and turned to her mother.

"I'm all packed, Maaa." She walked alongside the yellow rose bushes near the porch, pulling one toward her and bending to smell its fragrance. "Ouch!" She let the rose go and stuck her thumb in her mouth. She hopped up and down, raising puffs of dust in the dry morning.

"Let me take a look," Hillary said. Claire poked her thumb up in the air and pressed it against the other one. A drop of blood the size of an apple seed swelled out of the tiny puncture. Claire popped her thumb back in her mouth and jumped from one foot to another.

"Let's get a Band-Aid on that, and go check out how Gran's feeling after that fall."

"Let's take her a yellow rose," said Claire.

They knocked on the cottage door and at a cheery, "Come on in, it's open," Hillary and Claire entered. Claire thrust out the yellow rose she'd wrapped in a damp paper towel. "Smell it, Gran!"

Sarah held it to her face and inhaled deep and loud, then waved the flower in the air. "Thank you, my favorite! I'll get a vase in a minute." She laid the rose on the fireplace mantle, next to four short candles. She lit the candles and motioned them to come close. "Let's say a prayer for safe journey. It'll be too early tomorrow morning."

She nodded at the clear glass votives, each cupping a green candle. "I bought these green for Ireland. One for each of us." She nodded with a satisfied set to her mouth. "Keep up John's faith in the power of candles." She folded her hands and closed her eyes. "Just a silent prayer is fine."

They stood in quiet for a minute. Hillary shut her eyes. She loved the warmth of the candle ritual in memory of Sarah's late husband. Hillary focused on the journey and visualized their safe return home. All four of them.

Claire ran off to play outside while Hillary helped Sarah finish packing.

"I've been thinking," Sarah said, walking to her sideboard and pulling out some papers. "At my age, you never know."

"What?" Hillary said.

"I've made arrangements just in case, dearie. If . . ." She made the sign of the cross over herself. "Just in case, I took out some extra insurance." She laid the pages on the table, and rubbed her hand across the cover page. "In the unlikely event . . ." She rolled her eyes.

Hillary's stomach dropped as she realized what her old friend had done.

"If I should die over there, cremate me and take me back to St. Mary's, slip me in beside John. I set that up with the cemetery. Don't want to be a burden to you nor my own kids, not that they keep in touch."

Hillary felt faint but nodded. It was smart, really to think about things like that.

She spent the rest of the morning back at the big house, getting items crossed off the lists. When Claire came in, Hillary checked through her packing.

Their cats made it no easy chore getting clothes

folded and tucked into luggage, tirelessly fitting and re-fitting themselves into the suitcases. The two Himalayan Manx cats were grown up versions of those pictured on Claire's bedroom wall—fluffy black and white kittens cavorting in laundry baskets tied together with pink ribbons. Claire ruffled their long fur and lay alongside them in fits of laughter, giving Hillary the giggles, too. Finally, she had to shut the cats in the laundry room to finish packing.

She was grateful Roger would stay at the house, take care of the animals and get things ready for the Zinfandel harvest coming in September. She hoped to bring home another kind of harvest—the secrets of her father's family.

And have no encounters with Bridget's little hanky dolls—or ghosts of any kind.

CHAPTER 8

SACRAMENTO, CALIFORNIA TO DUBLIN, IRELAND

IN THE PREDAWN DARKNESS, Hillary steered north on I-5 headed for Sacramento's airport, feeling alert and grateful for last night's dreamless sleep.

The Golf hatchback was crammed with luggage, soft carry-on bags squeezed between Claire and Sarah in the back seat. Ed dozed next to her, trying to make up sleep lost over the past weeks on gang detail in Stockton. Pale daylight rose as she turned onto Airport Boulevard. It seemed odd that this sweep of fertile land was now an international airport. Granted, a few flights went directly to foreign lands and there were now two terminals. But still, it was a converted section of the vast rice fields of the Sacramento Valley.

Hillary was nervous about Sarah going through security and hoped she would get a break, courtesy of her stark white hair. But Sarah's hip replacement set off alarms.

"She's okay," Ed declared, pulling out his sheriff's badge. "I can vouch for her."

The TSA officer replied with a brusque shake of his head and guided Sarah forward.

"Can she," Ed said and nodded toward Hillary who was following close behind, "go with her?"

"No can do, partner." A female TSA officer, short and steely-looking, took over and motioned Sarah to follow her.

Hillary, Ed and Claire moved through the line without incident and gathered up their things from the belt along with Sarah's. They waited near a small bench where people were seated putting their shoes back on.

Hillary distracted herself by slipping on her reporter's mindset, scrutinizing the passengers moving by. There were a couple biker guys, heavily tattooed on their arms, necks and where their pale skin showed between leather jackets and pants. She knew most bikers weren't criminals. The real troublemakers often didn't look obvious. They appeared ordinary, like a short bald man, middle aged and focused on gathering up his brief case, newspaper and carry-on bag. What might he be up to? Had she and Ed talked enough with Claire about strangers? He'd always noted though that people the child knows were statistically more dangerous. She shifted her worry to what might be going on with Sarah and the TSA woman.

After minutes that felt like hours, Hillary was relieved to see Sarah reappear, clothes rumpled and glasses a bit crooked on her face. But she was laughing.

"Can't get me down," she crowed and collected her things set aside from the security belt.

"You're okay?" Hillary said. "What did she do?"

"Well, honey-girl, I've not had so much touching all over since John passed. Not all that bad, even if it was a woman." She closed her fist around the handle of her carry on. "Let's carry on, pun intended. Maybe find myself a man with the twinkle of a leprechaun over on the 'auld sod.' " She flashed a smile at a trim middle-aged man, striding toward the gates. He ignored her.

Hillary shook her head. Sarah, joking about getting a boyfriend? Sarah could handle the demands of travel, spunky as she was, but Hillary hoped there would be no elder romance to tangle with.

Claire scampered ahead of her father, her doll tucked under one arm and her pink carry on bumping along behind. She jumped over the narrow gap separating the tunnel from the plane, high-fived the flight attendant, and hurried down the aisle. Hillary's heart swelled with pride at Claire, so eager for her first flight.

Ed followed close behind his daughter and called out seat numbers. When they got to row 34, he reached out for her small suitcase and motioned her back to their row. Claire scrambled across the cushions to the window seat and lifted her doll for the view.

"See, Punzy, it's not scary." She turned back to her father, who was raising her suitcase to the overhead bin.

"Can't we get Green Bean out of there?"

"Let's leave Punzy out for the trip to New York. Then Green Bean can trade with her and take his turn for the flight to Dublin. He'll feel like he's going home then. How about it?" When Claire didn't complain about missing her stuffed leprechaun, Ed winked at Hillary.

He can always get her to do his bidding. Hillary squeezed herself into the middle seat so Sarah could sit on the aisle, able to get in and out easily. What a crush, she thought. Should have stuck to that diet better. Wish we could afford roomy first class seats.

Claire pulled down her tray table and set her doll on the edge facing the window. She pointed at the baggage carts speeding around on the tarmac. "Look for our suitcases." She finger-combed the doll's long loose hair. "You'll see clouds later on, all puffy and fluffy, just like your hair." She laughed and pulled off the hair tie from her own braid, dragging her fingers through her thick locks to loosen the waves. "We'll be like Rapunzel sisters in the sky!" She handed the scrunchie over to her mother.

"Careful not to get your hair caught when you close the tray," said Hillary.

Sarah unfolded her tray and reached across Hillary to get Claire's attention. "These are like what they used to put on the side of our cars at drive-in restaurants," Sarah said. "Bring us burgers and shakes. I'll have to show you pictures of that sometime, Claire-girl."

Hillary paid close attention as the flight attendants reviewed instructions in case of emergencies. She couldn't resist feeling under her seat for seat cushion straps in case they needed to become flotation devices. Horrible thought.

She made sure Sarah and Claire followed directions to put their tray tables up and fasten seat belts for take-off. When they reached cruising altitude, the captain predicted a smooth flight and turned off the seat belt sign. Sitting across the aisle from the three of them, Ed reclined his seat and closed his eyes.

Good. He'll need to be rested for what's coming, thought Hillary. Whatever that is.

When lunch was served on flimsy plastic trays, Claire sang out in delight, "Kind of tea party cups and things," she said. She poked through various sealed items, unrolled the paper napkin and set the plastic utensils in place. "Look at the apple juice!"

As Hillary reached to help, Claire gave the lid a big

tug and juice splashed in an amber fountain. The fragrant liquid poured down the edges of her tray table. Claire grabbed her napkin and started mopping at the mess. The tiny lunch tray slid off her tray table. She lifted the table and fastened it in a flash, then bent down. Before Hillary could stop her, Claire knelt in front of her seat, scrubbing at the wet carpet, her loose hair bobbing all over the place.

Suddenly Claire started shrieking, "Maaa! Help!" She was trying to stand up but her hair was caught under the seat. Her yelling drew a young flight attendant, who whisked away Sarah and Hillary's lunch trays and motioned for them to get up. Ed was standing in the crowded aisle and calling out to his daughter to stay calm.

Another of the flight crew joined them, a young man with a buzz cut, slim and fit. He scooted in next to Claire, who was hunched on the floor, holding her hair and whimpering. The young flight attendant was face to face with Claire and murmuring something Hillary couldn't make out. At the same time, he tugged gently at Claire's blond locks for a minute but then murmured up to his colleague in the aisle. "Get the scissors."

Hillary's heart was in her throat. Scissors. They wouldn't cut Claire's hair, would they?

"No!" Claire was screaming now, and Hillary could see her hand gripped tight around a hunk of hair near her cheek.

"Let me in." Hillary shook the shoulder of the young attendant.

"Don't worry," he said in a soothing voice. He turned to look up at Hillary. "Your mother is going to help you."

He moved back to make room for Hillary.

69

"Let go, honey," she said and reached in under the seat, feeling her way along the length of hair caught underneath. Claire's shrieks turned to moans. Hillary loosened the strands away from what felt like straps. In a matter of seconds, she had worked away the hanks of hair. She helped Claire to her feet and stood hugging her small frame until Claire pulled away and started laughing.

"Maaa, my hair was all twisted up. Not falling down from a tower, like Punzy's." Claire picked her doll up off the floor.

"Yes, this isn't a fairy tale," Hillary said. She blew out a huge breath and shook her head in unison with the gawking passengers.

"Emergency handled," said the young flight attendant as he handed over a stack of white terry towels.

The bald middle-aged businessman Hillary had noticed in the airport walked down the aisle, waited a few seconds for the mopping up and nodded without smiling as he moved forward, followed by several other passengers who'd been delayed by the uproar.

"What a brave girl you are!" exclaimed one matronly woman as she fondled her own braided crown of gray hair. Hillary gathered Claire's hair, braided it down her back and wrapped several pink hair ties around the ends.

In the hubbub of getting back to normal after the harrowing drama and then lunch, Hillary found herself more uptight than ever. This vacation was not starting out as much of a break. She looked across the aisle at Ed and mouthed *Want to trade seats?* He grinned, reclined his seat as far back as it would go, and closed his eyes.

"Claire," Sarah whispered when everyone was busy

with a movie or a game. "When are you going to get that hair cut?"

Claire sat silent, staring at her iPad mini and focused on Candy Crush's slippery excitement, ignoring the suggestion to cut her hair.

They changed planes in New Jersey, and this time were seated in four seats in the middle of the plane for the seven hours across the Atlantic. Hillary appreciated the pilot's announcement. "We're in the air on the way to 'air-rah,' " he boomed out. "That's how the Irish say Ireland, so you'll be in the know when we land in approximately six hours and fifty minutes."

Hillary got Claire settled with her iPad games. Ed and Sarah worked large print crosswords together. Hillary watched a documentary on Ethel Kennedy and her big Irish family, women having babies well into their forties.

Families. Grandad Patrick and his sister Fianna had sailed in the opposite direction back in 1928. Sailed was probably not the right word for the kind of ship they'd been on. Hillary felt sure Grandad never looked behind him to see the sunrise he was fleeing. He kept his eyes trained on the west, where he aimed his ambitious young self. His sister Fianna, too young to live on her own and too young to marry her sweetheart, was dragged along to California by her brother.

Hillary wished she had known this great aunt. She sounded like a bright and fiery relative, the aunt Hillary never had and still yearned for. The desire to learn about her Irish roots on her father's side certainly overrode her curiosity about her mother, who took off for Tahiti when Hillary was ten years old.

Horrible to imagine abandoning little Claire in three

years—that would never happen. The sins of the mothers don't have to be passed down the generations. Hillary reminded herself that her ideal family was right here with her.

She stared across the aisle out the small window into the dark and squinted for a horizon. There it was, a lighter shade of black, not yet gray, much less pink, but a narrow band of glimmer. The day peeked around the planet at the winged metal cylinder she sat in, Claire's bony arm wedged against Hillary's side.

Claire's arm flipped away from Hillary's ribcage in a jerky motion, and Claire cried out in her sleep, "Daisy!" She sat upright, leaned forward and yanked at her seatbelt. "Daisy, don't run so fast."

Hillary smoothed the few strands of hair that had come loose from Claire's braid. "Shhh." Hillary rubbed her daughter's thin shoulders and pulled her cable-knit cardigan up around her neck. "Shhh. Daisy's at home. She's home with her boy Rufus." Claire slumped back, her shoulders hunched up and returned to her dream. How awful it would have been if they'd had to cut Claire's hair.

Sarah was watching them. Even in the dim light, her cheeks were round apples astride her smile as she gazed at them. What a treasure to have Sarah as the grandmotherly part of their family. Hillary turned her head to study the sprawled out and sleeping form of her husband. Her heart warmed at the sight of him with his five-o-clock shadow and snoring so softly she could barely hear him.

Hillary turned again toward the window. They were flying into the dawn's pink fingers. This was the family she loved and would take to explore her heritage, thanks to Bridget's invitation to show them around

Galway. Hillary closed her eyes and dozed until the overhead lights came on and flight attendants pushed carts of warm wet cloths through the aisles, handing them out with tongs for the sleepy passengers.

"Prepare for landing," the chief steward's voice came blaring over the speaker.

"Here we are!" Hillary grabbed Ed's arm and splayed out the fingers of her left hand in front of his face. "The emeralds have finally made it here." She laughed and bent over to kiss him. He reached around to hug her with both arms as well as he could, strapped into his seat belt. "Happy belated honeymoon, Chickadee."

What would she ever do without him? Without any of them? She had to keep them safe.

CHAPTER 9

"MORNING, AILEEN." Seamus walked by his assistant who nodded but didn't look up. Her eyes were fixed on the computer screen, updating the site she'd created for his legal services, www.winInIreland.ie.

She's shut away in her own little world. If only Bridget kept to her own researched world, didn't want to invite everyone in.

Aileen jerked her head away from the computer and pointed to the date on her desk calendar. "The Millers from America are coming in at nine." Without waiting for a reply, she was back at her keyboard.

Walking into his office, Seamus barely noticed the sunlight flooding the room. He sat at his desk, got out a cigar and clamped his teeth around it. How to divert Bridget from her plans? She'd rejected marriage. He couldn't offer money—she was already rich from what her parents had left her so long ago. Besides, he wouldn't have the big bucks until the park opened and he got his percentage. Unless that other big deal cooking in Dublin came through soon. He rolled the cigar around in his mouth, not ready to light up. The young couple was coming in to sign conveyance papers on the house they were buying. They might not like cigar smoke in the air.

The big American hadn't liked smoke either. Seamus leaned back in his chair, sucked on his cigar, and recalled how they'd had to sit outside when Dermot came over that first time back in 2010. That way, Seamus could enjoy smoking his cheap cigars, but he hoped he could afford Cubans as soon as Dermot started the cash flow he'd promised.

They'd toured all over Connemara and then down south through County Galway to Ennis. Dermot liked the area around Gort and wanted Seamus to find him land for sale along the N18.

Seamus stood by the window overlooking Galway Bay. The last day of Dermot's trip they'd strolled the tourist section, visited the museum on the Long Walk and started an early afternoon pub crawl to seal their business deal.

Dermot had taken a liking to Bushmills whiskey. "Best find here—easy going and spicy even when the pub's outta ice," he said. "Not that different from my three ex-wives."

He raised his glass and toasted Seamus's pint of Guinness. "Sláinte." He laughed a low growl. "Sure, and it's grand to be Irish!" He reached out to pat the server. Lucky for him, he missed her or he might have felt the wrath of Irish goddesses all rolled into one woman's fist. "Finally here on Irish soil." Dermot belched under his breath.

"Ma would love to live here again." He sipped at his whiskey. "She still calls Galway home. Glad I found that website of yours, old man. Found a few shady types but was searching for a classy guy like you to help me jump through government planning hoops."

Seamus felt a glow of pride. Aileen had done a job on his real estate website, for sure. It had reached out around the globe and nabbed a big fish like this California developer.

Dermot swallowed the last of his Bushmills. "Want to help build up the economy here. If Trump can do it for golfers both in Scotland and here, I can manage a playland in Ireland." He signaled for another drink. Seamus was relieved that Dermot kept his hands to himself this round.

Dermot lifted his fresh Bushmills and inhaled deeply, puffing out his chest. "A small park should be a piece of cake after ten superstores, half dozen housing developments and that basketball arena, showcase of the NBA." He tilted his glass to take a healthy swig. "Finally ready to build the theme park of my dreams."

Seamus recalled he'd been surprised at how tipsy the uptight developer was getting, even starting to slur his words.

"Me Ma was a hotel maid, ya' know, in Los Angeles," said Dermot.

Seamus nodded, amused at how quickly Dermot had layered on a sort of Irish flavor to his speech.

"Took me to work with her and perched me on top a laundry cart while she pushed it up and down the hallways. She loves to tell the story of putting a towel over my head when her supervisor came by. A clean one, mind you." He sipped at his drink. "Towel, that is."

Seamus smiled at the strange image that brought to mind. He nursed his Guinness and listened to the man he'd begun thinking of as his benefactor.

"As I grew, I'd stand up in the cart and hand supplies to her. She started giving me nickels and dimes to pay for my help. Sure, she did." Dermot turned his glass in tight circles on the worn wooden pub tabletop. "I became quite the saver, washed out Green Giant Niblets cans and saved my coins in 'em." He started rolling the glass between his palms, making a swishing sound on the tabletop. The half-inch of Bushmills left in the bottom swayed in time with his motions. Seamus wondered what Niblets were.

"We lived just the two of us, Ma and me, in a motel across the freeway not far from Disneyland when it was new." He lifted his drink and drained the last of the whiskey. "Did'ya know that place is just 85 acres? And full of dreams come true. She kept me with her and dreamed of getting hired on there." When he set the glass down, he looked across the table, eyes watering.

Seamus remembered that moment, when it had hit him. Under his gruff surface, this titan in the business world truly loved his mother.

Like Seamus himself did. It wasn't Mam's fault their farm went to his older brother, who looked down on him and called him a fecking scumbag. Seamus worked to throw off the shame falling over his shoulders. He recalled whenever he made a mistake, his mam would laugh and sing out, "Shame on you, Seamus." She would hug him right away, but he wore invisible scars to this day. He felt a connection to the American.

A sharp tattoo at his office door startled him and brought him back to the present. Aileen opened the door and ushered in the young American couple, both blond and blue-eyed and fresh out of Notre Dame University. She introduced them as Harry and Millie.

"We're so glad to be here in Ireland!" Millie said.

"Yes, a resurgent country now, this land of ours. Welcome!" sang out Seamus, but he thought, welcome, for better or for worse.

CHAPTER 10

DUBLIN, IRELAND

HILLARY COLLECTED her credit card and put it back into her tote.

"Here you go." The Rent-A-Car man slapped a folder of contract papers onto the counter and topped it off with a map of Dublin.

Hillary pulled out the AAA map she'd already marked at home, highlighting the route from the airport to their B&B. "This one's just as good, yes?"

"That'll do the trick, lady." He nodded, his red hair flopping against his coppery eyebrows. Hillary had to laugh silently. The guy could have been her cousin with that hair.

His arm whipped out, pointer finger extended. "Your Astra is through those doors. Has a GPS and already set up with a seat fastened in for the little lady." He winked at Claire. "Should hold all four of you and your baggage if you don't buy up too much of the Irish to take home with ya."

She handed her map to Ed. "He's the navigator. If we get lost, we know who to blame."

Ed led the way out and they found their vehicle

within a few minutes. Hillary edged her way behind the wheel, situated on the right side of the car.

"Feels wrong," she muttered, less comfortable than she'd imagined she'd be. Ed directed her out of the airport and onto a crowded road leading into the city. It was a relief to see street signs in English as well as Gaelic.

She knew to expect crazy traffic, clogged with buses and delivery trucks pressing their size advantage. It was harder than she'd imagined, driving on the left side of the road. Her practice in the vineyard hadn't involved a vehicle with the steering column on the right and the gearshift down at her left. Despite the automatic transmission, she nearly hit a pedestrian in the few miles to the O'Malleys. She sighed with relief as she pulled into the parking area, paved over what must have been a front garden years ago.

Hillary waved at the brick two-story house. "We're here!" The four of them piled out and walked into a cheery entry, crowded with flowers. Oil paintings in frames of all sizes and shapes covered the red-flocked wallpaper. A musical tone echoed as the door shut, bringing plump Mrs. O'Malley in to greet them with exclamations of welcome. She called for her husband Wally to help get them sorted and up the stairs into their rooms.

"And what's the Wi-Fi password?" Hillary asked.

"Paddywagon," sang out Mrs. O'Malley, brushing back a few stray wisps of her salt and pepper hair. "Name of the outlandish tour bus outfit."

Hillary laughed. "I want to let my friend in Galway know we're here—in four pieces." She felt giddy from exhaustion mixed with relief they'd arrived safely.

"After you get settled, you come on back down. I've

got soda bread and cheese with salad fresh from Wally's garden."

Hillary saw to it that Sarah and Claire found their room and started unpacking before she joined Ed in their room. She sat on the edge of one of the twin beds and grinned at Ed. "Impossible to find king-sized beds here, not even doubles."

He flopped onto the other twin. "Have to go visit each other in the night." He laughed.

She pulled her laptop from her tote bag, got onto Wi-Fi and connected to Skype with no trouble. Bridget's smile beamed into the room and freshened Hillary's mood, if not her body, stiff and sore from the long flight.

"We made it!" Hillary shouted.

"That's grand! Thanks for checking in."

Hillary nodded and said no more, feeling almost stupefied from the long journey and relieved to make contact so easily with Bridget.

"Get yourself a burner phone and call me back in a day or two, love," Bridget said, "when you're over your jet lag. Got a new twist to tell you about."

"What?"

"Nothing." Bridget pursed her lips. "It can wait."

"Sure?"

"Absolutely! Go enjoy Dublin." She blew a kiss. "And, if you get a chance, take a look at the Famine Sculpture over on the Liffey dock. It will help you get on board with what I'm trying to do." She disconnected.

Hillary led the others downstairs to a table in the dining room, set with food and drinks. Mrs. O'Malley pushed open a nearby window. "The only air conditioning we have is this," she said. "Could be startin' another heat wave this summer." She shook her head and fanned herself with a folded *Irish Times*.

She opened up the newspaper, read the headline and nodded at Ed. "You're here for the Gangs Summit?" She frowned, her brows furrowing to a point. "Plenty countries could take a tip from what we've gone through here, ya know?" She handed the paper to Ed. "Good thing ye'll be working close with the Murder Squad over in Dublin Castle."

Hillary bit into the salad cress and other greens, glad for their cool crunch. She could feel her bones ache and hoped she could stay awake all day, as recommended for jet lag. Maybe it would be better to take a nap.

Sarah and Claire looked pretty fresh though, and Ed wore his usual never-say-die expression as he read aloud from the newspaper: "Garda Commissioner Martin Callinan claims there are more than twenty gangs active here and linking up with Russian mobsters." He set down the paper. "He's the keynote speaker at the Summit. We've got the same gangs over in our valley. Global crime all over the place nowadays."

"Lordy, lordy," Mrs. O'Malley said, "Callinan takes the heat from the loony fringe, to be sure." She shook her head, disappeared into the kitchen and returned with a carton of ice cream.

"Let's not start off your visit with such a dreary topic. Here's a treat from real Irish cows, a farm of my cousin's out in the countryside." She set down the tub and began scooping a creamy substance into glass dishes.

"Oooo!" Claire took the dessert with both hands and sprinkled on chocolate jimmies from a shaker in the middle of the table.

"I'm wondering if we should take an hour's nap before we explore the town," Hillary said.

"Some say no, but I've seen that be just the ticket," Mr. O'Malley replied. "After you come outside and take a peek at my shamrock patch, that is."

Clair looked up from her nearly empty dish. "Have you got four-leafed ones?"

He bellowed at her, "Aintcha seen shamrocks before, girl?"

"I'm ready. Let's go." Claire set down her spoon and jumped up.

Hillary was glad to see her respond to the gruff old man without fear.

"You youngsters go ahead," Sarah said. "I'll just sit and have another cup of this fine tea." She smiled at her hostess and held out her teacup.

Outside in the garden Mr. O'Malley led the way along a raised bed bordering the fence line. "I've got potatoes, sure, but sea-kale's my specialty," he said, bending down to rub some fleshy, collard-like leaves. "They're on the protected list along with the Bog-rosemary." He nodded at a patch of slender, dark green leaves, his chest puffed up with pride.

"We're heading south on Thursday," Hillary said. "What plants should we look for along the road sides?"

"That blasted Celtic Tiger and damned developers spawned some awful new roadways, took out much of the hedgerows." He tugged at his suspenders. "Thought they were doing a good thing taking out so much thorny growth, but na, we lost bushels of green along with jobs by the bushel."

Claire knelt and tapped a shamrock, causing it to bobble. "Can we grow these back home, Maaa?" She squinted up against the sunlight.

"We can," Hillary said. "Might bring us the luck of the Irish."

"That there's not belonging to us," Mr. O'Malley grumbled. "Was a curse put on Irish miners when they was in California, gold rush days. Insulting!" He huffed and poked around in the soil.

"Oops, sorry." Hillary had a jetlag headache.

"Too dry over your way," Mr. O'Malley said. "For shamrocks . . ." He looked at Claire. "We've got all the humidity here." He broke into a smile, looking like a proud mother hen.

"Okay," Ed said. "Wonderful. Now, let's go in and test out those beds. Time for a break before the night fun starts."

"The 'craic' we call our party time," the old man laughed. "Got to be careful the craic don't make you feel cracked in the morning." He winked. "But it's not the drug that sounds the same." He let out a blast of laughter that sounded more like a foghorn. "Just our way to say having fun. Out on the town."

Hillary felt too paralyzed to talk, her brain in a fog. "We've got to get some sleep . . ." She yawned. "Or we'll never make it no matter how much fun we can have."

A few hours later, the four of them gathered in the dining room for refreshments before their night out. Hillary sipped a cup of Bewley's Earl Grey to snap her awake. She glanced through the inside pages of the *Times*. A story with a Galway dateline caught her eye. Over the last week, the local Garda had been getting anonymous calls warning about a new ghost wandering the Long Walk. Several phantoms had been reported over the decades, a nun in black and later a lady in white, but this new ghost was said to be more malevolent and on the hunt for a victim. Tourists were in a tizzy of excitement over the rumors, which the Garda were trying to quash.

But wasn't Bridget's townhouse on the Long Walk, across from what had been the Claddagh fishing village? Was that the new twist Bridget was going to tell her about?

Claire pointed to the photo of a slim vaporous white figure, looking like a candle blowing in the wind. "Is that what we'll see tonight, Maaa?"

Hillary folded the paper and tapped Claire lightly on the head with it. "We won't know until we get on the bus, now will we?"

It had taken Hillary a bit of searching to find haunted places to satisfy little Claire's imagination. The GhostsRUs bus tour stopped at some of the most famous haunted sites, yet was all right for children. Sarah, too, had been excited over the online review describing the tour as a "Fantastic way to spend an evening if you are looking for a bit of craic with a dark twist!!"

Hillary made sure Ed would be along on this excursion, though she had zero belief in ghosts or such. Still, it was at night and in a strange place. It was all fun and games driving along Henrietta Street, lined with supposed haunted houses, until the bus headed toward the ancient Kilmainham Gaol.

The tour guide's voice lowered to a grating whisper as he warned the passengers to take special care when they were in the jail's chapel. "People have said they were pushed over, though I never saw it meself, so stand sturdy on your two good feet." He cleared his throat. "And mind you ignore lights flashing on and off when you get to the chapel and sounds of footsteps, banging and voices. We're here now, watch your step."

They got out of the bus and headed for the entrance

when suddenly two children about Claire's age stood stock still on the threshold of the old jail. They whimpered and hid their faces in their parents' trousers, refusing to go one step further.

Claire shook her head, rolled her eyes and walked on by. Hillary noticed she kept her hand in Ed's the whole tour inside the unoccupied prison where so many political prisoners had been tortured and executed in the courtyard. Hillary kept close to Sarah and was relieved that Sarah managed the cobblestones adroitly.

After they got back, Claire told the O'Malleys about the tour. "It was exciting and not scary at all," she said. "The poor ghosts are just trying to rest in peace." The old couple nodded and smiled.

Ed and Hillary helped Sarah get Claire tucked in to bed, her arms clutching Punzy and Green Bean. They watched her fall asleep seconds after her head hit the pillow. "Go on, you two," Sarah whispered. "We're fine."

Hillary fell to sleep the second she slid under the duvet on her bed. Her last thought was *I'm home.*

CHAPTER 11

DUBLIN, IRELAND

HILLARY SLEPT UNTIL TEN and woke groggy from jet lag, grateful she'd had no dreams. She looked over at the other twin bed, neatly made up, and for a second wondered where Ed was. It hit her he'd planned to slip out early and taxi to Dublin Castle to catch the Summit kickoff speeches.

She hurried to dress and get to the dining room where Sarah and Claire had just sat to start their breakfast. Hillary helped herself from the sideboard, taking a couple over-easy eggs from a platter next to another loaded with slices of thick bacon and fried potatoes. Hillary loved this kind of food. It was not far off from the corned beef hash she'd made a regular part of her diet before she got pregnant with Claire and was told to lay off salty foods.

Sarah poked at her sausage, grilled tomatoes, hot sliced mushrooms and what the O'Malleys said was black pudding. The black pudding was speckled with white dots that Mrs. O'Malley explained were the flavorful bits. It was a spicy treat, the ingredients of which she whispered were better kept a mystery. Claire was munching away at a bowl of Cheerios.

The O'Malleys tended to the roomful of guests. Mrs. O'Malley advised Hillary on how to get to a nearby shop for prepaid mobile phones and where to find the Hop-On Hop-Off bus stops for popular places they wanted to visit. After breakfast, Hillary tried to reach Bridget on Skype but got no answer. She'd try again later after she got a burner phone.

She made sure Sarah and Claire were prepared for a sightseeing day with layers of clothing in case of rain, and they headed out. Ed would meet them in the afternoon at the Guinness Factory, one tourist stop he'd vowed not to miss.

They hopped off the bus at the National Museum and wandered through Egyptian artifacts of all sizes hanging on walls and set out in cases. The exhibit next to that was titled "Irish Kings and Sacrifice." They soon became fascinated by the long narrow roomful of genuine mummified "bog bodies," arranged in glass cases. Clips of videos set into short towers in front of benches showed anthropologists explaining the discoveries and treatments of the ancient finds.

Hillary stared at a clearly deceased and leathery human being crouched into a fetal pose and lying on what looked like a bed of tar. Suddenly her attention was drawn to a conversation coming from around the corner of the glass display case.

"Bog Bodies. That's s'posed to be one of the features at the park that American is planning in the west, didya hear?"

"It's a sin and a shame, developers using suffering as a plaything."

"I've sent money to that group fighting that kind of Disneyfying our land."

"What a word. Disneyfy. Is that what that woman, Bridget something or other, is involved in?"

"Them big shots like Trump think they can stamp all over us, get their way, no respect for people and what we've gone through. Worse than the Brits."

Hillary peered around the corner to see who was talking but glimpsed only the backs of a couple of matronly figures walking off. Could they have been talking about her Bridget?

As they left the museum, the gray sky opened up. Instead of waiting in the rain for the hop-on bus, Hillary hailed a cab and jumped in, waving Claire into the middle so Sarah could get in last and not have to scoot across the back seat.

"I'm Michael," the young driver said.

Hillary asked to go to the Abbey Theater, and he threaded the taxi through crowded streets. "*Heartbreak Hotel*'s on now—you're a fan of Shaw?"

"We're not here long enough to catch any plays, but it was Yeats I studied most. I want to at least see the theater he started."

"You want to go west and visit Coole Park for Yeats. I was named after his son, ya."

"It's on our list," she said.

Michael drove through the crush of traffic alongside the Liffey, naming its bridges and pointing out boats for hire. He inched his cab alongside the broad quay sidewalk and approached a cluster of five or six skeletal human figures, scrawny shapes cast in bronze, coated now with a dull sheen from the rain. "Sure, there's our famine sculpture," said Michael. "Skin on bones, trying to get down to a ship and a chance at a better life. Starving, they were."

Claire stared unblinking at the life-sized figures clad

in rags, one man carrying a child about her size slung over his shoulder. "Maaa, why are they like that?" she whispered.

Shock numbed Hillary's face. This must be what Bridget had recommended she see.

"Maaa," Claire repeated. "What happened?"

Hillary was speechless.

"It's a sad tale, that," said Michael, glancing back at Claire. "There was hard times here a hundred years ago, when our potatoes got us sick."

Claire didn't say a word but her eyes got wider.

"There was other food, but the Brits kept it from us, was the truth of it."

"Troot?" Claire repeated the sound of the cabbie's word.

"Truth, honey," Hillary whispered.

Claire stared at the child cast in bronze, slung over the shoulders of a tall stick of a man wearing raggedy tatters. "Little kids like me starved?"

"I'm afraid so, girly," said Michael. "But they're trying to walk down to a ship." He pointed ahead in the direction of ocean-going vessels tied up some distance away on the dock. "Get on a big boat and cross the ocean."

Claire was silent.

Sarah's frown framed the sorrow in her eyes.

"Over to Canada and America, some went." Michael turned to nod at Claire. "But the starving, it's not happening anymore."

Hillary felt bad hearing the cabbie tell that half-truth to her daughter. Starving was happening still, though maybe not here. The intensity of Bridget's crusade hit her in the heart. How could Irish suffering be presented so it wouldn't turn tourist vacations into depressing drama? That's what Bridget was trying to do in the theme park. Hillary sighed, looked across the top of Claire's head at Sarah and shook her head.

Sarah slid her hand along Claire's back and patted her shoulder. The three of them sat quiet as Michael drove slowly along the dockside quay and turned to drive the couple blocks to drop them off in front of the Abbey. "Ye'll find happier sights, there. Should I wait?"

"No, thanks for asking," said Hillary.

She was relieved to find the box office and gift shop area open for business. Painted in dark tones of red and black, the place offered souvenirs and books on the history of the theater, now called a national treasure. An elderly clerk in the lobby was full of enthusiasm for its story.

"Yeats was one of 'em envisioned this here from when them writers gathered out in the west country," the wiry old man chortled, waving in the direction of a framed image of the bespectacled and bow-tied poet hanging on the wall. "He practically lived at Lady Gregory's place over near Galway. Have you heard of it?"

"Yes." Hillary leafed through a booklet on the counter. "I've seen pictures of the autograph tree at Coole Park and all those writers' initials carved into the trunk." She picked up another slim volume on the history of the theater.

"It's a huge Copper Beech, that one. Time and healthy bark's covering over the initials, so don't take too long about getting there." He chuckled and rang up her purchases. "Too bad Yeats' old square tower is closed to the public now. Stands high over a river, looking like something out of a fairy tale."

Claire's eyes sparkled. "Can we go there, Maaa?"

"You'd be safer on the ground, little miss," the old man said. "That tower is mighty tall."

"Tall as a castle?"

"Matter of fact, miss, it's called Thoor Ballylee."

Hillary noted he said Thoor as "Toor," turning "th," into "t" the way Mr. O'Malley had talked about them going to Cork on "Tursday."

"Now 'Thoor,' " he went on, "means castle in the Irish language." He leaned forward and looked straight into Claire's eyes. "Betcha didna know that!"

"I do now!" she said. "It sounds like the word 'tower!' I want to climb up inside and let down my long hair!" She pulled off the scrunchie holding her ponytail and shook out her thick blond waves.

"Looks like you've got your own Rapunzel stepped out of the story book." He nodded at Hillary. "Guess you're in luck the floods closed the tower."

Hillary gestured towards Sarah. "Between us, we keep this one safe."

"Good onya," said the old man, glancing at the windows fronting the street outside where rain had started drumming against the glass of the theater lobby.

"Should be cabs coming along soon," he said, nodding toward the street.

Hillary wished they'd asked Michael to wait. It was hard to know what to do and when. She had to get better at it and fast.

Hillary left Claire and Sarah in the lobby while she stood near the curb and tried hailing a taxi. She got soaked before flagging down a cab to get them the twenty minutes to the Guinness Storehouse where they would meet Ed in the lounge, seven stories up and boasting a 360-degree view of the Dublin skyline.

She was still shaking water out of her hair when she got off the elevator and spotted him, waiting in a pedestal chair at one of the tables scattered around the perimeter of the glassed-in rooftop lounge. The sky had cleared, and the whole city lay spread out in a colorful vista before their eyes.

"Here you sit all relaxed while I still need mopping up," she punched Ed in the arm, half playful, half mad.

"I didn't get myself any Guinness yet, Chickadee. Waited for you." He whipped out his handkerchief and blotted her hair. She pulled it into a damp bun at the back of her neck.

"I want mine in a bun!" Claire shouted.

Sarah plopped into one of the chairs and motioned to Claire. "Come here and let me put it into a bun, like Maaa's."

Ed headed for the bar in the center of the lounge where complimentary pints of Guinness were being served along with soda for young people and teetotalers. Hillary tagged along and watched a barkeep direct a stream of Guinness into a clear glass, the liquid swirling as if alive. Then the young woman behind the bar let it settle for a minute before she finished filling the glass and traced a shamrock in the foam by skillfully guiding the glass under the tap.

Hillary pictured the Guinness as an organic life form, boiling and toiling to escape the confines of the shapely glass. It was soothing to do nothing but stare into the mystery of the lively stout. They took the two pints back for Sarah and Ed to enjoy, and then Hillary strolled the picture-window perimeter of the room with Claire. Hillary read aloud some of the information painted onto the glass describing historic sites. Images of the illustrated old texts at Trinity College were alluring, and Hillary was sorry they wouldn't have time to see those sacred books. They completed the circuit of the lounge and sat down beside Ed and Sarah.

"Does the Guinness here taste better than back at home?" Hillary asked.

Ed raised his eyebrows and licked his lips in approval, but Sarah looked sleepier than she'd been after the ghost tour the night before. Hillary got herself a half-pint of Guinness and a Sprite for Claire.

Hillary sipped at her Guinness, relishing the thick creaminess of it, and started to relax into the vacation she had yearned for. She gazed out into a bright Irish sky but when she thought of Bridget working away out west in Galway, she couldn't help but feel guilty enjoying herself as a carefree tourist in Dublin.

Later, they took the glass elevator back down to the main floor and puttered around the gift shop, looking for lightweight and flat items that would fit into their suitcases like Guinness bottle openers and aprons.

On the way out, a display of old glass bottles caught Hillary's eye. They were mostly beer and stout bottles but included a few for whiskey and wine, as well. "I never heard of wine being made in this cool climate," she said to a young Guinness guide who'd come up next to her.

"Just a bit of it, now and again. All in the south," said the guide, with a bright smile.

"Look here, Ed," Hillary motioned him over. "This whiskey bottle." She pointed to it and took a photo with her cell camera. "It's called 'Writers Tears.'"

Ed stood at her side. "You know all about those, Chickadee," he said, putting his arm around her waist. "We'll try and find a shop where it's for sale."

She kissed him and nuzzled his five o'clock shadow. Keep tears stored up inside a bottle—good idea.

CHAPTER 12

DUBLIN, IRELAND TO CORK, IRELAND

"AFTER BREAKFAST we're driving down south. I heard that's Ireland's wine country," Hillary said. She bit into a slice of black pudding, beginning to like the spicy sausage. "You know we run a vineyard in California."

"Wine. Humph!" retorted Mr. O'Malley. "Honey mead is one thing, but that German lad moves over and thinks he can grow grapes here."

"Well, mostly," she smiled, "it's to visit the museum down in Cork. I've got an appointment with a genealogist."

Mr. O'Malley glared at her. "That's the Cobh Heritage Center, if you want to call it by its right name," he huffed. Hillary noticed he pronounced Cobh as "cove."

He shot a black look at his wife. "Cork's a grand place except for getting taken over by that Apple Factory."

"Now Wally, don't get your blood pressure up," Mrs. O'Malley sang out and looked at Hillary. "He's just stuck in the old times, is all."

He scowled. "All that malarkey about Celtic Tigers and the money trail. Ha! Damn Apple got taxes so low, they broke the government bank. No money to fix anything now."

"Wally, give Apple a slice of credit." Mrs. O'Malley fanned herself with a folded newspaper, then tapped it against her palm. "Just read there's over four thousand people working in their Cork plant. Got to count that a blessing."

He took the paper from her and threw it into a waste bin near the coffee and tea service. "Not gonna fill up them ghost estates, empty with wild kids running amok in 'em."

"Ghosts?" Claire's eyes widened, her spoon of Rice Krispies halfway to her mouth. "Kids my age?"

"Not that kind of ghosts, dearie." Mrs. O'Malley stirred the scrambled eggs in the chafing dish on the sideboard and smiled at another family who'd come into the breakfast room. "He means houses built when times were good but later jobs ran out and then no one could afford to buy. Empty houses now. Not for you to fret over, little chicken." She stood aside so the new-comers could help themselves to the buffet.

Claire's face fell. "Oh. Not real ghosts." She carried on crunching bites of cereal.

"Now, if it's ghosts you're wanting," Mr. O'Malley's piercing blue eyes took on a sparkle, "not far from Cork is the white lady of Kinsale." His bushy eyebrows fell as he closed his eyes to narrow slits and started in on a legendary ghost tale. Claire sat entranced.

Hillary went up to her room to call Bridget on the new prepaid phone but got no response, so she planned to try and Skype later from the Cork guest house.

Ed took a turn driving on the wrong side of the road. Hillary kept her Triple A map handy and made sure the car kept on a southwest direction towards Cork. It was great that Ireland was small enough to get most anywhere in a day. Finally she would walk in the footsteps of Grandad Patrick and his sister Fianna. The day was overcast, but no rain was breaking though. Yet.

Hillary had booked them into Harley's Guest House, partly because it was near the harbor and partly due to its free Wi-Fi. After they checked in, she got Bridget on her laptop screen right away. But she wasn't looking sunny today.

"Everything is fine here, except…" Bridget's faced squinched into an apple doll look.

"Except what?"

"Not that big of a deal, but…" Bridget's eyebrows shot up, smoothing her looks back to nearly normal.

"But…" Hillary was used to prompting people to talk. The work of a ghost writer was to surface the truth.

"Well, I'll show you when you get here."

"Can't you tell me now? Get me prepared?"

"How about if you take Seamus's phone number—he can tell you in case something happens to me."

"What! Something like what happens to you?" Hillary got a fluttery feeling in her belly.

"It's just those little dolls I told you about. I stopped the paper but they are still coming every morning. Out on the roadside. Still a handkerchief wrapped over a cotton ball in the center, the corners looking like a skirt."

"What?"

"Not to worry. I think it's just a joke."

"How can that be funny?" Hillary waited. Silence was often better than questions.

"But now, they look different." Bridget let out a hoot. "So stupid. The rubber band making the neck has a thread wrapped on top of it, a silky white thread. Like for doing embroidery."

"Holy Mary," whispered Hillary. "Why don't you call the Garda?"

"It's just so silly. I don't want to give them any more power."

"Them? Who?"

"We can talk about it when you get here."

"I'll get Ed to look into this," said Hillary, breathing hard.

"Just take down Seamus's number in case you can't reach me." Bridget gave out numbers as Hillary scratched them down on her notepad. "I'll give you some other names tomorrow. Sean Mor and his son—part of the Broome family."

"You watch out, hear me?" Hillary said, feeling sick and nervous. "I'll call you later."

After they got settled in the guesthouse, they strolled alongside Cork Harbor. Red petunias in baskets atop poles everywhere added a festive note, but Hillary's worries about Bridget stayed on her mind. There was a park with playground equipment, so they got lunch from a little market and set Claire loose in the park. A sign announced Dermot Connolly Developers had donated improvements to the park, crushed tires for the ground, making it slightly spongy and resilient against little bodies in case of falls. There was that name again. Dermot Connolly.

Hillary sat on a slat bench and studied the waters of Cork Harbor. This was the very spot where the Irish had departed for their ocean voyages, hoping for better lives. The stories were dramatized in the Heritage Center, and Hillary was excited she would be learning more. They would go to the museum as soon as Claire used up her energy. She scampered up a tall ladder to the slide, stood at the top platform and pulled off her hair tie. Shaking her hair over the edge of the railing, she yelled, "Look, Maaa, I'm Rapunzel!" She flung herself onto the slide, whizzing down the slick surface, and repeated her circuit a half dozen times.

Each time Claire stood at the top platform, Hillary held her breath, amazed at the athleticism of her child. Soon Claire was off to the monkey bars, seizing each rung, hand over hand with ease. Hillary relaxed. A little monkey she was. Lean and agile like Ed.

Hillary was grateful Claire hadn't got a pudgy body like hers. She was still trying to lose the same ten pounds over and over—with a hope of losing ten more after that if she could keep the first ten off. She'd gained forty pounds when pregnant with Claire, and only lost thirty, so she now packed around a hundred and ninety despite trying to jog an hour every day along the vineyard roads. When she could get to it. The nursery rhyme from childhood echoed in her mind. Jack Sprat's wife could eat no lean. And so between them both, they licked the platter clean. Ha. Too clean.

Hillary's reverie framed the sight of Claire on the swing, getting pushed high by Sarah's muscular arms. What an inspiration. Sarah was in good shape for being in her sixties. She drove herself to the Lodi senior center five days a week and made use of the gym. Plus she played duplicate bridge to keep her mind sharp.

Too bad about those kids of Sarah's. Out on the East Coast ignoring their mother except at the end of every October when they'd fly out for Day of the Dead. They would take Sarah up to Sacramento's St. Mary's Cemetery and put sugar skulls and other Dia De Los Muertos decorations on their father's grave. Sarah said she never wanted to move east, so that's how their family worked nowadays. Neither of her kids had married or had any grandchildren for her, so she relished being with Claire.

A piercing shriek yanked Hillary from her musing. Claire lay in a heap, the swing arcing gently above her. Hillary ran over. Sarah pulled a big handkerchief from her skirt pocket and handed it to Hillary. "Don't think it's bad, she was just slowing down from the ride."

Hillary dabbed at a scratch on her daughter's cheek. Claire batted her eyelashes and began laughing. "Scared you, Maaa!" She jumped up and ran over to her father, raising her arms to get lifted into his. He swung her around as if they were dancing on the spongy surface.

Good thing she's such a lightweight, Hillary thought. Where had this daredevil daughter come from, so unlike Hillary and Ed with their cautious ways of facing the world?

"She's got my spunky spirit," said Sarah. "Good thing I always carry one of John's big handkerchiefs." Sarah folded it and slid it into the pocket of her denim skirt.

Hillary shook her head. "Let's get out of here before she runs back and falls off the top of the slide ladder, cushy ground or not."

The narrow sidewalk forced them into single file for the few blocks to the Heritage Centre. Hillary's heart jumped to her throat a couple times as Claire hopped off and on the narrow walkway. Hillary was surprised at how large the place was. Emigration was just one part of the museum among others showing the story of Cobh's connections to the Titanic and the Lusitania. Hillary was relieved that Ed, Sarah and Claire would have plenty to keep them occupied, including a gift shop that advertised books and toys for children.

She checked in at the genealogy section for her appointment, fluttery inside with excitement. What would her online donation have resulted in? A tall balding man offered her a smile, a handshake and a chair next to his desk. "Call me Brian," he said. "Good to meet you. We appreciate your donation. I've got your family tree printed out." He smoothed papers on his desktop and ran his fingertip along ruled lines, tracing connections of Grandad and Fianna to her own name. Hillary tingled with the warmth of belonging.

"Claddagh Village is one of my specialties, being from Galway." Brian pointed to dates in the middle of the nineteenth century. "This is back when the potato blight hit and Matthew Broome emigrated to America.

"In 1847, he and his wife Grania packed up their brood—five of their eight children not yet starved to death—and sailed off to Canada. They survived 'ship fever' and settled in Boston. Later their grandchildren moved to the Irish community in San Francisco."

Brian gave a firm nod. "The Broome family name is now inscribed on a brass plate added to the Wall of Dedication here in the Centre, part of the permanent record of the courage and spirit of your family." Brian's gave a warm smile as he handed her an Emigration Certificate.

Hillary held the fancy document with trembling hands.

"But Fergus was the only one of your people . . ." he said. My people, thought Hillary. My people.

"The only one to leave back then in the potato famine—or great hunger as some call it," Brian continued. "Early in the twentieth century there was a massive outbreak of tuberculosis in Claddagh Village and the whole place was deemed a public health hazard." He produced black and white photos of shabbily dressed figures standing in front of whitewashed cottages with thatched roofs and few windows.

Hillary nodded, knowing what he would say next.

"During that time your great grandmother died and the young Patrick and Fianna left for California. Claddagh Village was destroyed by order of the Galway Council."

Destroyed. Hillary sat wordless and tender with sorrow.

After Brian finished up his presentation, Hillary staggered out of the Genealogy office and wandered to find the café. She craved a cup of French roast coffee but settled for Irish breakfast tea to help bring herself back to the present. Ed found her, holding a half-empty cup of tea and staring at her family tree packet.

Ed scooted a chair close and reached around her shoulder to give her a squeeze. She closed her eyes and clutched his hand, clinging to it before she spoke. "Grandad and Fianna's sailing was probably not so bad, but the ones coming over before . . ." Hillary choked up. She sat in silence while Ed looked through the papers.

"Maaa! Look what Sarah got me from the gift shop," shrieked Claire. She perched a six-inch puppet wearing a wispy bridal gown on the edge of Hillary's cup. "It's the White Lady. Her husband was shot the night they got married!" Claire made the puppet push Hillary's teacup toward the edge of the table. "She was sad all her life and came back as a ghost to push people down stairs." She looked at Hillary with huge eyes. "But it's not true, is it, Maaa?"

"Some people believe in ghosts, but I think they're

just stories for exciting entertainment," said Hillary. She picked up her cup and drained the last of the cold, sweet tea. "Let's go over and see the emigration exhibit. It will be a little sad, but it's what happened here more than a hundred years ago. It shows what your Great Great Great ...," she frowned. "I haven't got all the 'greats' sorted yet, but it's what some of them went through."

She led the way out of the café and down the wide hallway to the exhibit.

Hillary felt at one with the crush of tourists, silent and rapt, watching and listening to productions of how it must have been for the Irish preparing to emigrate. A touching ballad told the story of a man imprisoned for stealing corn for his starving family and on his way to servitude in Australia, leaving his wife alone in the fields. Some of their dramatized farewell speeches were interspersed by wailing from family and friends at gatherings called "wakes." The emigrants were gone forever from their homeland—same as dead to those left behind. Posters on the black walls called the sailing vessels "coffin ships" since so many died on the crossing.

"Coffin ships," thought Hillary. Boats full of ghosts.

She heard a man whispering to his family that he'd heard of cannibalism among the starving Irish but wasn't surprised there was no mention of it here. Hillary thought of the Donner Party Memorial back home in the Sierra Nevada. They had mentioned that aspect but not given it much space. It seemed likely that could have happened during the Irish famine, she thought, but put it out of her mind.

The four of them spent an hour looking into the dim alcoves of the exhibition. Hillary studied photos of emigrants in the years between 1925 and 1928, looking for what might have been a young brother and sister pair. As far as she knew, there had been no photos of Grandad and Aunt Fianna leaving for America after their mother died. Another sad mother story, she thought. But getting sick and dying wasn't the same as abandoning them.

Not like the way her mother ran off on her.

CHAPTER 13

CORK, IRELAND

HILLARY FELT DRAINED when they got back to the guesthouse but checked on Bridget who answered the call immediately.

"We saw so much history and suffering at the Cobh Center," said Hillary. "Is that the same kind of education you want to see in a Pot O'Gold memorial museum?"

"It's getting there but what the Irish went through deserves more honor and respect." Bridget raked her fingers through her long black hair. "They've barely scratched the surface at Cobh, showing the causes and degrees of misery, wretchedness, torment." Bridget's words burst from her lips across the Skype screen, as if in an animated film. "Tribulation. Affliction. Soul-wrenching anguish."

Hillary sat hushed by the passion in her friend's voice.

"And how many know the difference between the terms 'famine' and the 'great hunger?'" Bridget's gaze seemed to be looking far away into a haunted past.

"We had enough food in Ireland. It just wasn't distributed to the poor," she said. "A famine is when there isn't enough food. 'A Great Hunger' is what it really was. Thousands were forced to starve." Her shoulders slumped. "I'm pretty sure some died on the roadside . . ." She blinked back tears. ". . . in front of my own house."

"I never knew," Hillary whispered.

"But in America," Bridget carried on suddenly, "details of the Donner survivors are told in the Sierra Nevadas, in Sutter's Fort and even in novels like *River of Red Gold*."

Hillary recalled the time she and Ed stopped at the Donner Memorial on interstate 80 on the way to Reno. She'd heard of holocaust memorials Germans had erected, too, repenting sins of the past. Bridget was on the right track, the decent track.

"All we are asking is for the developer to put up a tasteful but honest memorial in Pot O'Gold." Bridget held the ghost doll up to the Skype screen and jumped the cloth figure up and down, the silk threads around its tiny neck flying. "But no word from them. Instead, these dolls, from God knows who.

"Even worse," she went on, "one of the planning councilmen was found strangled at the old Blackwoods House. The owner wanted to renovate the estate as a tourist attraction." Hillary felt a clammy pit in her belly as her friend rushed on with details. "Evidence points to ghosts of maltreated servants in the past, but . . ." She frowned.

"What kind of evidence?" asked Hillary.

"Old yellowed newspaper articles with their edges blackened by fire, one on the body and the other nailed to the front door."

Hillary didn't know what to say.

"And even worse, my big old computer's been wheezing and whooshing at first when I boot her up lately. Got to get a techie out here, help me back up the files, see if we can prolong her life. Seamus can't help. He has to be away Friday and Saturday on a land development deal in Dublin."

"He's sure close to developers," Hillary said.

Bridget laughed. "We both got involved trying to get the economy booming again. That's how we first met."

Hillary wondered about this Seamus and if he was really right for Bridget. She hadn't brought up the wedding again, so Hillary didn't mention it either.

Now worry for Bridget crept over her, and after they disconnected, Hillary got the old rosary out of the inside pocket of her suitcase. She fingered the pale pink beads and thought about praying for Bridget's safety.

But Hillary was out of the habit.

CHAPTER 14

GALWAY, IRELAND

LATER THAT WEEK after the hubbub of the day and Aileen had gone home, Seamus lit up a cigar. He opened a window and stared out over the bay. The waters shimmered and brought to mind the edgy finish to the story Dermot told over the hours of their pub crawl that night way back then.

"When I got old enough to ask where me father was, Ma put me off, told me she had stories for when I got older." Dermot flagged the waitress for another round, and shot a questioning look at Seamus, but he shook his head and kept a hand over his stout glass.

Dermot set his fresh drink on the table and stared at it. "Said Da was a musician and actor out on the streets of Galway." Dermot gestured toward a group of actors in ratty costumes out on the street, delivering some sort of theatrics on the other side of a low fence separating the pub tables from the street.

"Like those." He grinned, the warmest smile Seamus had seen from him. Seamus nodded back, feeling the connections.

"She was one of Da's buskers, she said. They put on street theater for tourists and collected more money in their plumed hats than other acts did. Da played roles in plays all over the country, and after a few years got the backing of friends to go to Hollywood and try out for the movies. Can you believe it?" Dermot took a swallow of whiskey. Seamus nodded and waited for more of the story.

"Ma told me she came over with him to Los Angeles and it didn't take more than a year for her to get pregnant and for Da to fail at breaking into films. With a screaming baby as all the push he needed, me da took off and we never heard from him 'gin." He polished off his Bushmills and narrowed his eyes to dark slits.

"Ma never would tell me his name. For all I know, could be one of them clowns, face all made up crazy like ..." He thumbed in the direction of a cluster of street performers howling at each other and poking at passersby. "And who needs him?" Dermot slammed his empty glass onto the table and made the flimsy iron legs jump.

Seamus turned away from the window and sighed, remembering how he'd felt stunned with the rest of the drama of Dermot's story.

"I was in love with making money and with Disneyland. Ma got a job there, a second job, and learned how to sneak me into work with her there, too. I was small and a bit on the unwashed side, and didn't make it to school much. Got bullied whenever I tried school, and made up me mind to be somebody anyway, school or no school." Dermot got red in the face and started breathing fast. Seamus offered him a cigar, thinking it might calm him down, but Dermot wanted none of it.

"Kids called me Der-dummy. Guess we can see who were the dummies from that school." Dermot signaled for another round of drinks. "Ashholes," he slurred and glared at Seamus. When the waitress came, he gave her a pinch on the bottom whereupon she howled for the owner, a stout bald man who came running with a scowl on his face. Dermot yelled out: "Think I'm some kind of ugly American? Fools. You'll treat me like a king when you see the jobs I bring."

Seamus flushed with embarrassment at the memory. They'd gotten thrown out of the place. But they had sauntered down Shop Street to the next pub with out-door seating.

"This's another thing I love about Ireland," exclaimed Dermot. "You're never far from a bar." He ordered fresh drinks, and kept on talking.

"I got Ma to tell me stories about Ireland—the secrets I could tell you—might not be much truth to 'em." When their drinks arrived, Dermot toasted Seamus, glass to glass with a clank. "By the time I was in my teens, I was busing in the hotel restaurant and graduated to sweeping streets at Disneyland." He thumped a fist against his chest. "And then on the construction crew helping build additions to the park. Did I tell you? That place is on just 85 acres."

He stared at Seamus, a faraway look in his eyes. "Want to bring Ma home, set her up in a nice house near fields fresh and green, and show her what I've accomplished." He finished off his drink and pounded his fist on the table. "And by God, I will!" Tears slid down his cheeks. "Wanna call it Kathleen's Pot O' Gold."

Seamus had felt it an honor back then to be helping Dermot, who'd seemed a giant of a man. Things were so different now. Shame flooded over him. What a fool he'd been then, and now he was a coward, too.

CHAPTER 15

CORK, IRELAND TO GALWAY, IRELAND

THE BOOM AND THE CRASH and the tinkle of glass. She clamped her hands over her ears. The screaming got in. She wriggled down to the foot of the bed. Yowling hit her. Her heart fluttered like the wings of a hummingbird inside her body, paralyzed in a case of ice. Frozen and frenzied all at once.

Hillary woke drained and drenched in sweat. She lay still in the quiet morning. Was that breaking glass?

Silence. Ed must have left to catch the bus back to Dublin. She worried she could have been crying out in her sleep and hoped she didn't waken Sarah and Claire in their room down the hall.

She rubbed her eyes, stretched and got up to part the white curtains. The window glass was spotless. She tapped on it, testing reality. If the glass broke, she figured it wouldn't make the crystalline sounds from the dream. No way to find out. The field beyond sported a battered old boat hull, blackened and put out to pasture.

At the wall sink, she washed her face and blotted it dry with a scratchy towel. The towel smelled of the outdoors, the fresh and salty air. Trembling, she began spreading on her makeup. It always calmed her after a nightmare, masked her pain as well as her aging skin. Maybe she should try leaving it on all night to keep the dreams at bay.

She yanked up the covers on the twin bed and sat down. Leaning over, she pulled her prepaid out of her tote and thumbed in the number Bridget had given her.

Seamus picked up immediately, and after she told him who she was, he said, "Oh, sure, Bridget told me you would be coming."

"Hi. It's good talking to you, too." She waited but he didn't respond. "I just wanted to make sure I had your number right." She was glad she'd not mentioned her part in Bridget's wedding plans.

He sounded nicer when he asked for a favor. "I'd like if you'd get up to Galway soon. I'm away on business this weekend and worried over Bridget."

Maybe he *is* the right man for her after all, she thought, and told him they were planning to arrive that night.

"All right, then." He disconnected.

Sure isn't much of a talker, Hillary thought. Hard to figure.

After breakfast, Hillary packed up quickly and got them on the road toward Ireland's rugged west coast. Sarah was acting as navigator with Hillary's highlighted Triple A map in her lap. It had served well on the way to Cork, so Hillary didn't bother to turn on the GPS.

The air was cool with a hint of sun breaking through the clouds. In the back seat, Claire busied herself reading ghost stories out loud to Punzie and Greenie from *A Night in Terror Tower*. It amazed Hillary how talented the girl was with various voices since she'd been watching that *Haunting Hour* on TV. Hillary wished she could write for children like Stine did—and make the super scary thrilling but bearable. For kids like Claire anyway. Maybe she would turn out to be an actress.

After a few hours, Hillary pulled into the Cliffs of Mohr, the biggest tourist stop along the rugged Burren coastline. They followed the signs from the parking lot crammed with cars and tour buses over to a building carved into the side of a hill. Sarah and Claire hurried off to the Ladies. Hillary purchased a cup of Bewley's and spotted an empty table in the crowded gift shop café. She sat down to call and check on how Ed's summit was going.

"Walk in the footsteps of the gang members and be them," he said with enthusiasm. "That's the slogan for today. Tonight, we're busing up to the Irish Republican Army headquarters."

"Sounds so organized. How can that help in San Joaquin County? Your gangs are scattered all over." Hillary blew on her hot tea and motioned Sarah and Claire over to the table.

"The Garda's come up with a variation of what we call community policing in the States. When they started the program, they got to know outlaws deep down as people—it took years. But it worked to cool off the fighting here—it's not such an issue anymore. Really odd, but it's out of the box and nothing we're doing now is working."

"Watch out in IRA territory. You're there to learn how stop crime, not to become victims. Can you hold for a sec?" She gave a twenty euro note to Claire and told her to go treat Sarah in the cafeteria line. "Ok, I'm back." She glanced out the window overlooking the parking lot. "So, be careful, darling. We need you."

"This isn't some Showtime TV series. I'll be fine, Chickadee. You keeping our girls under control?"

"The trails here edge along cliffs hundreds of feet over the ocean. I'm trying to keep Sarah and Claire indoors as long as possible. Wish you were here to help keep a rein on them."

"Might have to buy a knit leash if we go out to the Aran Islands, tie it around Claire's neck, keep her from getting too near that drop-off at Dun Aengus." He laughed.

Hillary shuddered as Claire ran off.

The three of them mounted the broad white stairway, Sarah doing well going up. At the top there was a railing bisecting the path, so adventurous trekkers could walk unfenced along the sheer drop side. Hillary made sure they walked inside the railing but Claire kept standing on the bottom rail and waving both arms in the air. The wind was strong and made for a clear view of the Aran Islands and Galway Bay. Hillary's nerves were screaming all the way along the path, but she kept a grim smile on her face. When they'd gone about half a mile, a young boy ahead of them jumped outside the railing and slipped on loose rocks. As he stumbled down to a ledge below the trail, his horrified mother screamed for his father to go back and get help.

Hillary immediately turned them around. "We've got to get on the road, get to Galway before dark," she said. "I need to check on Bridget." She made it a game to keep hold of Claire's braids as if she were a pony as they walked back single file inside the railing along the cliff edge and down the steep and broad stairway. Sarah took the steps slowly, her brows knitted in concentration, the downhill looking like it was bothering her knees and hips. She said she was fine, but Hillary feared walking along the cliffs may have been too much for her.

Hillary threaded the car out of the parking lot. She slid in a Clancy Brothers CD and headed north in the warm afternoon, humming along with the familiar tunes. At Too-ra-loo-ra-loo-ra's soothing Irish lullaby, she glanced over to see Sarah nodding off. The high-lighted map slipped from her lap to the floor. We'll be okay, Hillary thought, the signs show we're headed to Galway. Let her get a nap in.

Hillary glanced back at Claire, unnaturally quiet. She was asleep, too, her books fallen off to the side. The Irish music played softly in the background as she rolled along the road. She tried to imagine what the countryside would have looked like years ago, what it must have been like for people to dig all those stones out of the dirt and form the short rock walls dividing the land into green rectangles of pasture, dotted with cattle here and sheep there. This is the getaway she had yearned for, immersing herself in the rolling green hills of Ireland. She sat up straighter. Not good to get too relaxed.

Some time later, Sarah jerked her head and woke up. "How we doing?" She took her glasses off and rubbed her eyes.

"I think we're okay but the road looks like it might be narrowing down," Hillary said.

Sarah grabbed the map off the floor, smoothed it over her lap and ran her hand along it. Hillary slowed down and hit the buttons, rolling down all four win-dows to let in fresh air.

Claire leaned out of the window. "Maaa, I can almost touch the bushes! They have thorns! Like the roses at home!" she screeched.

Sarah turned to the back seat. "You watch out, sweetie," said Sarah. "We don't want any bloody fingers in the car." She turned back to face Hillary and lifted the map. Hillary slowed to a near stop and looked at where Sarah was pointing. It was about a half inch away from Hillary's yellow highlighted marker line.

"I'm afraid we missed the turnoff to Galway," said Sarah. "I'm sorry."

"We'll get straightened out," Hillary said, turning on the GPS but knowing her only option for the time being was just to keep going on this road.

She drove through the dense air, feeling hot and weary when suddenly she came upon what looked like a street fair, close by the roadway. Tents of red canvas were set up. She parked near the festive scene, and they headed straight for a booth selling shaved ice. As they walked along biting into blue frozen slush in paper cones, Hillary was surprised to find nothing for sale but empty plastic bottles in all sizes and shapes.

"What are these for?" she asked a vendor.

"Don'tcha know, lady?" he replied with a smile. "You're in the holy city of Knock."

"Knock?" Where were they?

"Sure. Church is over that way." He turned toward his right and gave a nod.

"What church?"

"St. John the Baptist. The blessed Virgin herself showed outside on the wall when we needed her bad. Over a century ago, it was. You're in time to catch the four o'clock mass. You must have the luck of the Irish." He laughed loud and long.

"The holy city of Knock?" Hillary's jaw fell open. "Let's go see what it's like." They sucked up the rest of their mushy shaved ice, tossed the empty paper cones into a bin and turned the corner to find a small church. They walked into the gift shop. A half dozen posters told the story of the miracle at Knock.

It had happened on an August day back in 1879 when many were suffering from poverty, evictions and emigration. The Virgin had appeared on the back wall of the church, part of a tableau that lasted three hours. People came bringing their sick. The miracles that took place over the years stunned everyone and it had been declared an official shrine by the Vatican. The apparition wall was now enclosed in a sort of second sanctuary built around it.

Hillary led the way to one of the pews arranged facing the back wall of the church. Claire and Sarah sat side by side, holding hands. Hillary surreptitiously took a photo of their hands—a gnarled old one and a smooth young one. She thought of the wedding photo of Ed and her hands, too, her left one with the emerald wedding ring showing front and center.

Hillary surveyed the scene. A stone sculpture of the Virgin Mary stood wearing a white cloak and a bright crown, her hands in prayer and her eyes raised heavenward. St. Joseph and St. John as white statues stood there, too, all of them to the left of an altar with a lamb standing on it. On the back wall were six angels, three on either side of a white cross behind the lamb. Hillary felt like she had back in the Lodi cottage, when Sarah lit candles for their safe journey. Let us get safely to Galway, Hillary prayed.

When they got outside in the courtyard, Claire asked about the statues on the back wall. "Which one is God?"

Hillary felt shame heat her whole body. She hadn't taken Claire to mass, had neglected to go herself for nearly ten years although she still prayed to Holy Mary at those hard times when her father died and when she miscarried that first baby.

"Well, the lamb up on the altar—"

"Is that what you call that table with the cross behind it?"

"Yes. So, the lamb stands for Jesus, the Son of God. You know, who was born on Christmas day."

"Why is he a lamb?"

"Well . . ." Hillary looked at Sarah, who chimed in, "At Eastertime, you know how we have bunnies and chickens and little lambs? The lamb stands for a pure white being that is willing to die for the sake of the people, to save them."

"But where is God?"

"Well," Hillary resumed her part. "You can't see God because God is a spirit."

"Just because you can't see or touch something, doesn't mean it isn't there," said Sarah.

"Like the ghosts in stories." Claire nodded firmly.

Hillary exchanged glances with Sarah. "Sort of like that, yes. We can talk more about it later."

They walked around the open courtyard. Although it was now after five, the long days of summer in Ireland provided plenty of warm sunshine. On the hedgerow perimeter of the courtyard stood a dozen fountains with tile backdrops.

Hillary put two and two together to realize what the empty plastic bottles were for—to fill with holy water from a fountain. It couldn't hurt to carry along with them, so she went back into the gift shop and bought four small plastic bottles, one each for them and one for Ed.

"Here," she gave a bottle to Sarah and Claire. "Let's get some holy water to protect us."

Hillary filled hers and waited for Sarah and Claire, standing at a different fountain, to finish theirs. The old woman and the girl laughed out loud until they saw Hillary with a stern look. "Shhhh. This is a holy place. Quiet." Hillary nodded in the direction of a couple of monks standing guard at the hedgerow.

It's always a good thing to have protection, she thought, even when you don't think you are going to need it. Hillary shuddered as a cloud passed overhead and blocked the sunlight. She walked out of the courtyard and tried to phone Bridget but no answer. The worried words from Seamus echoed in her mind.

Hillary went back into the church's gift shop and asked for a newspaper. They carried only the dated tabloids from the Vatican. Nothing local or even national, the petite nun behind the counter said with an apologetic smile.

She went back into the church and lit a candle for Bridget. "Holy Mary, Mother of God," she prayed to the Virgin, feeling lost after a long absence and hoping Mary would welcome her back as a prodigal daughter. She knelt in silence until Claire and Sarah found her and urged her to get up and get going.

They walked back through the colorful tents selling empty plastic bottles. Now she knew what they were for and was amazed to see some of them in gallon sizes. Had she poured herself enough protection?

Hillary turned on the GPS and entered the address for the Quinn's B&B. As nightfall darkened the cloudy sky, she made her way along the R339, grateful it was not yet raining. She pulled in and parked next to a small van with a sign painted on the side advertising the B&B. No one was in the entry, so she rang the counter bell just seconds before a woman with dark hair in a long bob came running in from the back.

"Welcome!" she cried. "Failte! A hundred welcomes! I'm Loretta, Loretta Quinn."

"Missing the turnoff made us late," said Hillary, "but finding Knock was worth it."

Sarah added "Almost," and plunked herself onto a bench upholstered in bright red velvet. Claire climbed onto the bench and lay her head across Sarah's lap.

"Ah, the holy city—grand isn't it?" Loretta walked around the counter to motion towards the open front door. "You got parked all right?"

"Yes, and I want to stay parked. I'm exhausted from the driving," said Hillary. "One reason my friend recommended your place was that you're a five-minute walk to the city centre."

"We can help out there, too, our van is your transport—if you need it. Kind of a tourist taxi we like to provide our guests. We only charge you for the petrol."

Hillary signed them in on the guest register and got Claire and Sarah settled in a room near the back garden, glad they were all on the ground floor. It was after ten before she wheeled her carry on into a room at the front, with a bay window, not certain when Ed would be there. She'd booked a room with twin beds, sure he'd be getting away from his summit meetings in a day or two. Her arms throbbed from the long day of driving. She plopped on a bed and phoned Bridget but it went to message.

She stretched, raising her elbow above her head and reaching down to the middle of her back to lock hands.

It felt wonderful to hold each stretch for the count of twenty seconds. She lay down on top of the white duvet and thought about getting ready for bed. The room was stuffy and she got back up to crank open the two side windows. Suddenly, a taxi pulled into the front parking lot.

Ed had arrived!

CHAPTER 16

THE NEXT MORNING, Hillary tried to reach Bridget again but no luck. She left a message and then went out to join Ed, Claire and Sarah at a table next to the front window. They took turns getting seconds from the colorful spread of food set out on the sideboard. While they ate, they watched tourists march determinedly by, towards downtown Galway. The street was lined for blocks with roomy old homes now converted into B&Bs. There was a sign on a small hotel nearby, advertising live music in the bar from eight to ten at night.

Ed nodded toward the street. "It'll be another hot one," he said. "Good thing our windows crank open. No AC here, not even electric fans like in Dublin."

Sarah had taken to carrying a souvenir fan, which she now spread open and fluttered in front of her face. "I've got that problem solved." She turned the fan in Claire's direction. "Rent it to you for a good price, little girl." She laughed.

"I'm cool," said Claire. "I've got a body born for the heat, Maaa says." She turned to Hillary. "Can we go to the big park today?"

"Maybe we want to get out early, walk down and look for old Claddagh village." Hillary took a swallow of coffee.

Outside the window, not two feet from their table, she saw a short man flicking a lighter and holding it to a cigarette. Sarah looked at Ed and raised her eyebrows.

"Reminds me when I used to smoke those little cigars," he said, expanding his chest and inhaling deeply as smoke drifted through the open window. Claire started coughing, and Sarah fanned the smoke away from Claire's face.

Hillary asked Loretta if the man was a guest and if she could suggest he move to the other side of the front door.

"Sure, now. That guy arrived late last night. I'll ask him for ya, it being breakfast and all."

Hillary sat down, feeling uneasy. Loretta went out and talked to the man, who cupped his smoke in his hand and strode off toward the street, taking a drag on the cigarette when he reached the sidewalk. He stomped off in the opposite direction from tourists headed towards downtown.

"Well, we haven't made a new friend there," said Sarah, folding shut her fan and letting it fall to her side. "Hope we don't run into him much."

After finishing breakfast they walked down the street toward town. The road had colored flags strung overhead along the way to old town. They headed towards Galway Bay, looking for Claddagh Park. Hillary was both excited and sad she'd be getting to see the site of the fishing village Grandad had emigrated from. On the way, they passed shops crammed with tourists hunting for souvenir bargains.

They went into the Galway City Museum set back

from the Long Walk. On the second floor, Hillary stayed longer than the others at a window looking down on what had been Claddagh Village. The window glass had been painted to show where parts of the old fishing village would have been. Photos under glass were positioned as if a person were looking across the quay at the little village in its day.

Hillary felt chills run up and down her spine as she looked at the photos. A few rows of whitewashed one-story cottages each with a front door and a single square opening for a window—none looked like there was any glass pane in it. All were thatched with straw in various stages of deterioration. That's the way Grandad had lived before he and his sister Fianna emigrated just after their mother died in the tuberculosis epidemic. Soon after that, all the traditional cottages were burned to the ground to stop the spread of the disease.

So sad they had to demolish it all, thought Hillary. The lack of any of it still standing touched her heart. Nothing was left but the few photos. These pictures might tell many stories if only she had more clues. But there were not even any ruins—all the secrets were floating in the air, invisible.

Later, Hillary ducked into a shop that was advertised as the home of the Claddagh ring. A slim bespectacled man sat behind a narrow counter, a loupe fixed onto his right lens, working on the innards of a watch. Hillary made a quick circuit around the shop admiring the rings, earrings, necklaces. They were pricey, as she'd already learned from websites.

"Excuse me, sir." When he didn't look up, she said, "What do you have that a man could wear?" she asked.

With his head still down, he muttered, "A real man can wear anything in here."

Hillary felt stung, but pressed on. "I mean are there plain gold bands with a Claddagh symbol inside perhaps?" She had fantasized something like that would be available and had played around trying to slip her own wedding band onto Ed's ring finger to get a sense of his ring size.

The jeweler stood, taller than Hillary had expected. "Yes, mam," he said, suddenly taking on a friendly tone. "Only playin' with you." He laughed and pulled out a tray from under the counter, loaded with what looked like plain gold and silver bands. "These are not traditional, no, but I made 'em up after Americans started asking same as you." He took one from the tray and held it so Hillary could see inside the band. There it was—a miniature perfect heart, a hand on each side of it and topped by an itty bitty crown. A micro-claddagh symbol. So fitting for Ed's hands of friendship, heart of love, and his crowning loyalty.

"I've got a nice price on these, as well." He pointed to a price sheet taped to the counter. "Just a hundred euros."

Hillary looked outside. Ed and Claire were still at a tee shirt shop across the street and Sarah was standing just outside the jewelry shop. "Come on in," Hillary called out.

"What do you think?" She motioned to the tray of rings. "For Ed?" She looked at the jeweler.

He tilted the band so Sarah could see the tiny engraved Claddagh symbol on the inner surface. "There are a couple stories of its origins, but it's been the traditional Irish wedding ring for centuries." He grinned as if he himself had invented the design. "Our shop was the original maker, most trustworthy shop in all Ireland, we are."

Sarah pulled her glasses out of her purse and set them on her face to peer into the ring. "Ah, mighty tiny but seems . . ." she raised her head to look at Hillary, ". . . seems perfect for your Ed. Plain on the outside but full of romance and royalty on the inside." She nodded. "Yes. But what's his size?"

Hillary pulled her ring off and held it out toward the jeweler. "This ring fits his little finger," she said. "Can you figure what his ring size would be from that?"

"Done plenty," he said. "Can put your initials inside, give me an hour more. Mighty nice band you got here, lady," he said, nodding. "Good workmanship." He slipped it over his ring sizer. "He wears a size nine, I figure."

Hillary glanced outside and saw Ed and Claire across the street, souvenir bags in hand. "I'll come back in a few hours," she said. "You'll have his ring ready, in a box? Inscribed HB and EK?"

He nodded. "Run along. I'll see you later this afternoon."

For dinner that evening, the four of them strolled to the hotel for the advertised special—grilled salmon. A bearded man with a guitar who introduced himself as Jimmy came into the dining area, set up with speakers and a sound system. As they enjoyed their meal, along with a few pints of Guinness, they got into the music.

Hillary asked for "Galway Bay," not really expecting the man would know it, since she realized that what Americans sang as Irish tunes were often not authentic. However, this man did know the song, and Hillary sang along with him, helped with lyrics she'd pulled up on her smart phone.

After that, Jimmy began plucking out mournful notes on his guitar. "Here's a real Irish song for ya," he said before he started singing. It was not easy to follow the meaning of the words about a man who'd stolen corn to feed his family and had been convicted and sentenced to exile in a foreign land. The song was a plea from the man to his wife to raise their child with "dignity." Sarah and little Claire were both near tears as he repeated the sad lyrics a second time.

Dignity. How dignified could anyone be if they were starving to death.

The guitarist ended his ballad. "Athenry, ya. It's not too far from here. My home," he said. "I play in the pub there on nights when I'm not here. Come visit a real Irish town if you've got a car and the time."

Hillary took that as a perfect cue. "Speaking of time and things that are really Irish," she said, winking at Sarah and turning to Ed. She drew the tiny box from her tote. "Here's a true love token from your real Irish woman."

She handed the box to Ed, who sat with a slack jaw in surprise. "What?"

"Open it!"

He pulled the lid off the box and stared at the gold band sitting in its little satin slot. "What have you done?"

"Well, I didn't get you a ring back when we ran off to Reno." She smiled and pulled the ring out. "But here's a belated one on our overdue honeymoon." She took his left hand and held the ring at the tip of his finger. "Let's see if it fits, my man."

It slid on easily. They gazed at each other with smiles

growing wider by the second, then kissed a long kiss as Sarah and Claire laughed and clapped their hands.

Jimmy'd taken in their joy and announced his last tune of the evening was for them. "When Irish Eyes Are Smiling," he said. "It's perfect for tonight." The other diners lifted their glasses towards Hillary and Ed and the room was full of song.

They strolled back to the B&B in the warm dark evening, Sarah and Claire skipping along ahead of the two of them. After they crossed the bridge, Hillary heard a rustling and turned to study the trees. She elbowed Ed who was looking in that direction, too. "See anything? Anyone?"

He narrowed his eyes for a few seconds. Then he whispered, "Only shadows. Let's stay away from trouble. It follows us so close anyway." He hugged her and said, "Let's go take a look at my ring in the moonlight from our bay window." He kissed her on the neck. "Hate it that I can only stay an hour, but I have to get on the road to Dublin and prepare for the daybreak sessions."

She shivered, feeling both hot and cold in the Irish night.

CHAPTER 17

GALWAY, IRELAND

AFTER ED LEFT, Hillary hit the remote and turned on the bulky old TV, sitting atop the battered armoire in the corner. A newscaster was commenting on a prank someone had pulled, stuffing crumpled *Irish Times* into empty Levi's and a white shirt and setting the "body" out on City Hall lawn, holding a sign warning about ghost estate taxes. She felt hollow in the belly, a gnawing emptiness spread through her.

She called Bridget but no answer. Why? Where could she be?

Loretta was still working at the registration desk. "Must keep you busy, running this place," said Hillary, propping both elbows on the counter and resting her face on her fists.

"Paperwork aplenty, now it's folks sending in online reservations." Loretta stood and shook her head, her black hair brushing her shoulders. "Can't complain, tourists coming back real regular now." She yawned and stretched her arms high. "What can I do for you? A cup of tea? We've got chamomile."

"No," Hillary said. "It might sound silly, but I haven't been able to reach my friend Bridget on the phone. You know, Bridget Murphy. She recommended you. I wondered if you might have an idea of why she wouldn't pick up?"

"Ah! Bridget. Doing grand work promoting our All-Irish small businesses. Well, let's see." Loretta tucked a loose strand of her long hair behind her ear. "I know she's under a load of pressure, fighting that developer and all, God bless her. We've thought of going to one of those planning meetings to support her but not had time yet. I have written letters to the editor, though." She pulled open a drawer and slid a ledger book in. "I heard she takes midnight strolls in her downtown neighborhood. Could sound scary but it's pretty safe, being just down the road from our city museum."

Hillary felt a bit foolish. "So she should be back home around 12:30 or so, you think?"

"Most likely, yes. I wouldn't worry about her, she's a fighter, that one. Go on now and get some rest."

Hillary took off her makeup and smoothed on some night cream. She read for a few minutes before she nodded off.

She was riding salt waves at the foot of a cliff, smashing into a vertical wall, her fingers spread out like starfish, feeling for cracks in the stony wet wall, wiping at the slippery surface. Icy water tossed her about like a limp shirt in a washing machine, thrown up and down, crumpled over and over. Each time she reached the top, buoyed up by some wicked current, she spotted a bridge in the distance, a bridge to dry land. Then rubbery claws grabbed at her toes and pulled her down, flooded with terror. Ropes of seaweed encircled her neck. The harder she tugged, the tighter they squeezed.

She woke up gasping, the front curtains blowing into the room and brushing against her face. She jumped up, ducked under the curtain and cranked one of the windows closed. A shadowy figure danced behind the B&B van and disappeared into the night. Her heart skidded in her chest, her palms coated with sweat. She had to wipe her hands on the duvet before she could crank shut the other window.

Her phone showed the time as four thirty-four. More than an hour before dawn. She tried going back to sleep but it was no use. She got up and dressed, then checked her map of Galway. It wasn't all that far from the B&B down to the Long Walk—just looked like a few blocks past the city centre. But it was still dark outside. And cold, too. She pulled aside the curtain, half expecting the shadowy figure to reappear, but saw nothing except the shiny reflection of wet car tops in the front lot. It was starting to rain, too. Just great, thought Hillary.

She stepped to the door and gripped the brass knob, pulling downward to minimize squeaks and turning it slowly, surprised at how quiet it was. Out in the entry, light from the back rooms spread a pathway she followed to find herself in the Quinn's kitchen. Loretta was bent over an open oven, pushing in a pan of something, her apron clutched around the pan as a potholder. A couple heavy saucepans sat near each other on the cooktop, their lids jiggling in muted harmony. The smells of browned sausages reminded Hillary she'd not eaten a proper dinner the night before.

"Good morning to ya," whispered Loretta, standing and brushing her apron down smooth over her jeans. "We like to get the meal ready ahead of time for our guests. Coffee?" She pointed to a thermos jug on the counter.

"What a Godsend you are," Hillary said. She poured herself a cup. "You must never get much sleep."

"Time enough to sleep when they roll the old sod over me face," Loretta said with a firm nod. "I like being up and at 'em as you might say over in the States. What brings you to my kitchen so early?"

"I wanted to come to Ireland to rest and relax, work with Bridget on my family history, but . . ." Hillary added lots of milk to her coffee.

Loretta lifted a lid and poked a long wooden spoon into one of the pots, giving it a few stirs. ". . . but?"

"Well, I had a nightmare and think it's because I can't get hold of Bridget."

"Ah! That's what's after worrying ya." Loretta untied her apron and hung it on a rack by the back door. "Let's go now, get in the van. Just take us a few minutes to drive over and check to see if her car's in front."

"Great!" Hillary gulped a couple quick swallows of coffee. "Would you?"

"Sure. If the car's there, we'll just bang on the door nice and loud. It's getting near daylight—she'll be up working already, if I know her. If the car's not there, then—"

A man pushed open the back door, a tall man with a bushy red beard that looked like it might have been grown to make up for his shiny bald head.

"Liam, can you keep an eye on the porridge for me?" Loretta reached for her windbreaker on a hook next to the apron.

"Where you off to?" He smiled at Hillary and stuck out his big hand. "Welcome. I'm the hired help around here." He nodded with a twinkle in his eye.

"This is Hillary. They came in late, night before last. We're just running down to the Long Walk, check up on something. I'll take me mobile and call if we need anything."

Hillary stopped by her room to grab her rain jacket. Once in the B&B's van, it was light enough for her to make note of the direction they were headed. Loretta explained that Liam had lost a good deal of his night vision, so he only drove the van in the daylight. She pointed out the city hall grounds to their right. "That's where some jokesters set out a tax protest, fools!"

Then she drove by the town square. "Eyre Square, we all call it. But it was renamed John F. Kennedy Memorial Park when your president came over years ago, in the early sixties it was. I was a babe and me mam loved to tell the story."

Hillary's worries grew as they rode along. What if Bridget was fine—just had her phone turned off or a dead battery? She would think Hillary a crazy American, paranoid or something.

Loretta drove alongside a small harbor and circled around a block to drive past a row of houses fronting the bay waters. "These are the Long Walk places. Pretty pricey here right across from the old Claddagh Village."

She pulled into a parking spot parallel to the row of houses. "See." She pointed along the sidewalk in the direction of a house further down. "Her car is there. That red Audi. Let's go knock on her door."

They got out and walked a few feet on the slippery pavement, hoods pulled up and hands over their eyes like baseball cap visors. After a few steps, Hillary stopped and stood perfectly still. "What's that?" she whispered.

Loretta had stopped, too.

Hillary could see a bundle lying on the sidewalk, the

size of a body bag duffle, getting pummeled by the rain. From the end closest to her, some kind of white streamers spilled out on the concrete, interspersed with strands of long black hair.

She was transfixed, unable to take the next breath, let alone another step in the direction of Bridget's house.

It couldn't be.

PART II

Things fall apart; the centre cannot hold.

W. B. Yeats, "The Second Coming"

CHAPTER 18

DUBLIN, IRELAND TO GALWAY, IRELAND

SEAMUS DROVE LIKE A MADMAN along the motorway. It struck him odd to see sunlight pouring all over the M4 on this day, so dark for him now.

Hillary's phone call had thrown him into a crazed state. His hands trembled on the steering wheel as he neared the side of a bright green Paddywagon tour bus. A blast from its air horn refocused his attention.

Jaysus! The divided roadway had kept him from a head-on collision. He overcorrected to the other side of his lane, and glanced up at the blue sky above.

Clouds formed in his mind and heart. He should never have left Bridget alone, should have insisted he move in with her, could have conducted his business deals by Skype. Didn't need to be running off to Dublin all the time. He floored the accelerator even though it was too late to save her.

He'd planned to be on the way home from his Dublin meetings, looking forward to their Saturday together. Bridget had hinted he would be happier than last week when she'd sent him away with his spur-of-the-moment cigar band ring wadded into his palm. He leaned over and poked around in the glove box, feeling for the tiny crushed band while he kept half an eye on the motorway. He was glad he'd kept the silly thing. Even though now it could never be. Never. He blinked back tears.

The wail of a siren yanked his attention back onto the road. A glance in his rear view showed lights flashing from the blue bar atop a vehicle sporting GARDA painted across the hood. The cop wasn't passing him but instead locked in on his tail. Seamus steered over to the side of the road, and the police car pulled up behind.

"See your licence, mate?" The motorway cop was young and fresh faced, dressed in a luminous green jacket, so bright it yanked Seamus's mind to the problem of the moment. He nodded, pulled out his wallet and flipped it open to his licence, showing through a plastic window opposite his favorite picture of Bridget. His heart pounded in double time.

"Pull it out for me, would ya, please?" The Garda pressed his lips into a tight line.

Seamus slid the licence out and handed it to the cop. He couldn't help thumbing the outline of Bridget's face. Tears blurred his vision but he blinked them back.

"Saw ya' sliding around in your lane. Going awful fast, you were, ya?" The Garda handed the licence back to Seamus.

"Sorry, officer." Seamus was stunned. He couldn't let the cop know his girlfriend had just been found dead, murdered. He might not have been allowed to keep driving in that sort of emotional state. Or did cops care about that?

"Where you off to in such a hurry?"

"Galway, sir. Back to my office. Been meeting with clients in Dublin, real estate deals, getting the economy rolling again, sir." He was amazed at how quickly he could transform himself into a polished professional. All law-abiding business. He started to feel the sweat forming under his white shirt.

"Mighty heavy foot, you've got, mate." The young officer nodded his head and pulled out a citation pad.

"Officer, I'm one of you. On the side of the law. No need for a ticket, is there?"

"Exceeding the speed limit is a serious matter," the young man said as he began writing, pressing firmly on the pages.

Seamus's heart raced. Now his underbelly was exposed. He'd be a certified law-breaker, he who used to strictly enforce the laws. Back then. He rubbed his cheeks, trying to cool the hot shame flooding his face. Get hold of yourself, man. It's not like you're going to gaol.

"Slow down, Mr. Hanrahan." The officer tore the top copy off his pad and handed it over to Seamus. "Our country needs you to get home all in one piece."

"Yes, sir." He slipped the ticket into his wallet, forcing himself not to look again at the photo of Bridget. Don't think about her now!

Back on the motorway, he felt numb. He had to summon every ounce of strength to hold himself together, walk the edge of this horror that was his own fault, not let himself snap on over and tumble into the loony bin. He forced his mind to focus on details of the land purchase contract he'd been working through back in Dublin. He watched as the Garda followed him for a kilometer or so then turned off on a side road.

Seamus drove along holding his mind blank until he saw a sign with arrows pointing toward the M6, toward Galway.

Galway. His home… and hers. Until now.

Hillary said they'd found her in front of her house on the Long Walk near the museum. Stuffed into a laundry bag, white tie streamers around the top.

He fought against dark visions clamoring in his mind but lost the battle. Seamus visualized her trim figure as she sprinted down the Long Walk, same as she did every night. She must have been easy to stalk.

Seamus could almost feel the muggy August midnight air as Bridget jogged around the block from her house. Someone must have stepped out from hiding and mirrored her pace. Seamus envisioned her turning to look into the killer's eyes. He must have looped the white tie over her head, crossed one side over the other and yanked them in opposite directions to strangle her.

Seamus steered with one hand. He reached up with the other to clamp against his throat, pushing against the cords of his neck, feeling for what she must have gone through. That bastard. Must have kept a grip and counted out the seconds. Seamus felt for his own carotid pulse. He imagined he could feel it slow to a stop. The bastard probably ran through the alphabet twice in his mind, give it plenty of time. Maybe three times. Made sure Bridget wouldn't live to identify him.

Why hadn't he protected her? He felt a dark cloak of remorse for what he had failed to do. It was like that blanket of fog falling over his shoulders when he was ten and realized what it meant that he was not number one son. Born at the wrong time. Not good enough to inherit the farm. Ashamed of something he couldn't control. That must have been why for every little misstep he made, his mother said, "Shame on you, Seamus."

Bridget never did. She called him "Shay." He would never hear her clear strong voice again. Never. Never.

Tears rolled down his cheeks before he could hold them in check. Another siren yanked him from his worst imaginings. He glanced in the rear view to see a police vehicle pulling past him, on the way to nab some other bloke.

Seamus shook his head and slapped his face hard, trying to focus his attention. He concentrated on getting safely down the M6 past Athenry and into Galway, looking for the address Hillary had given him.

He clenched his jaw and straightened his shoulders. He had to put his professional face back on and set up a time to read the will. Bridget's last will, testament to what? His failure.

CHAPTER 19

GALWAY, IRELAND AND THE TOWER

HILLARY PICKED at the ploughman's lunch set out on the sideboard. She was surprised anyone could think of eating a bite after hearing about the murder. That morning Claire had cried that she wouldn't get to meet Auntie Bridget, but Sarah had comforted her with stories about heaven. She described her husband John, who Claire had never met either, and told about the dream messages he sent her with tales of lovely flowers and little animals playing under the rainbow bridge.

"I won't get to be her flower girl," said Claire. "She won't get to be a bride."

"Now, she's surrounded by flowers and humming-birds of all colors," Sarah said. "Remember the little lamb at the church at Knock?"

Claire nodded.

"Auntie Bridget is safe there in heaven with that lamb and the lion and the others all in a peaceful place."

Now Sarah and Claire nibbled at plates of cheese and bread with pickles. The longer Hillary sat there, the sicker she felt. She wondered if her nausea was the horror of Bridget's murder. Or something else she couldn't let herself think about.

What was happening at the coroner's? How would Bridget be taken care of? Once Ed got back he could go find out. Seamus had sounded nearly speechless when she'd called him. She hoped he was safe on the roads. How long did it take if you drove straight through from Dublin?

The B&B entry hall melody broke into her thoughts and drew her out from the breakfast room. A slim and fit looking man stepped into the entry. "I'm Seamus. You must be Hillary."

His blue eyes took her breath away. Those eyes, magnetic and piercing like she remembered cousin Teddy's. No wonder Bridget had taken up with this man.

He reached out for her hand. "She was so looking forward to your visit."

Hillary's eyes brimmed with tears.

"Not sure if you knew," he said, "but she and I were, um, dating. I was hoping it would be more than that, but . . ." His words trailed off.

Hillary's voice stuck in her throat. He never knew Bridget was planning to accept his proposal. She threw her arms around him in a spontaneous hug, but he stood rigid. She pulled away and looked at his face, immobile.

The man seemed to be all business. "I was also her solicitor, what you call in the States, her lawyer. You were in her will, did you know?"

Hillary felt stunned at this news, and she stared wordless as he went on.

"Most of her estate goes to a fund to help people in poverty buy houses. But she left you her research on

145

the Broome family, along with some money and money for your Great Aunt Fianna's son and grandson."

What was wrong with this man? How could he be so unfeeling to carry on like this?

"They've not . . ." He choked up for a second and looked away before he carried on. ". . . heard. About what happened." He cleared his throat. "They've got no phone out there—don't believe in 'em. So—"

"Out there?" Hillary felt glued to the spot.

"Over at Coole Park. Got to go tell them to come into town so we can have the reading of the will. They're caretakers—like to keep their cottage the way it was when Lady Gregory ran the place."

Suddenly his face broke from its firm countenance and he stood slack-jawed, shaking his head. "Back in the old days," he said. He turned away to look out the narrow window flanking the front door. Hillary was frozen in place, listening.

He turned back. "Bridget used to talk about her good old days. Seems she never got over losing Teddy."

Hillary nodded.

He sighed. "I couldn't measure up." His shoulders slumped. "When her parents died so soon after Teddy, that wiped out her family. She kept their pictures on her mantel." He shook his head. "She had no other relatives."

Hillary nodded, remembering Bridget had called her a sister friend.

"So she felt connected to the Broomes even though most of you were out in California except for your cousins here, Sean Mor and his son Sean Og."

"Mor and Og?" Hillary hardly recognized her own voice, grown faint with sorrow.

He looked at her and gave a half chuckle at her expression. "Mor and Og, the way you have Senior and Junior."

Hillary felt herself broken into pieces. "I wish I'd gotten here sooner," she whispered. "Bridget always sounded . . ." She lowered herself to sit on the little entry bench. ". . . so self-sufficient." An ache filled Hillary's chest and spread out through the veins in her arms. She should have tried harder to reach Bridget. That might have thrown her off her midnight walk, could have saved her life.

Seamus cleared his throat, all business again. "I can do the reading of the will as soon as Fianna's son and grandson can come to my office. Do you want to go out to find them with me?"

Claire burst into the entry just then. "Go out where?" she asked, grabbing Hillary's hand.

"Who's this little lady?" Seamus smiled.

Hillary introduced her daughter, and Seamus gave a bow in response to Claire's big grin. "Go to a big park in the country. Two little girls lived there with their grandmother, Lady Gregory. They wrote a book—*Me and Nu*," he said.

"Nu?" Claire asked. "You mean 'Me and You?'"

Seamus chuckled. "Well, one of the girls had the nickname of 'Nu,' so that's where the title came from. The book tells about their adventures in their grandmother's woodlands."

Hillary took a deep breath. The room seemed to shimmer around them as if this were not reality. But it was and things had to be taken care of.

Seamus led Hillary and Claire to his car along with Sarah, who didn't want to be left behind at the B&B. They drove twenty minutes through the rolling countryside, quiet inside their own thoughts.

They stopped at the Coole Park gift shop to use the

bathroom. On the way out, Claire spotted a children's book for sale. She picked up a copy and handed it to Hillary. "Please, Maaa? It looks sweet." Hillary got out her wallet and set some euros on the counter.

A slim woman with a brown bun at the nape of her neck took the money and pointed to a stairway. "There's a nice set of rooms up there, dear, showing what life was like for those girls here at Coole Park, back in the early twentieth—"

Seamus cut her off. "We'll have to return another time. Right now we need to find the caretakers. It's a legal matter."

"Ah, our Seanies have cranked up their old Ford and gone over to the castle."

"Castle?" Claire was bright eyed and hopping up and down.

"Ballylee. Yeats Tower. We call it a castle," the woman said with a proud smile.

Hillary felt a wooden sadness at this occasion to be visiting the home of the great poet. Once they were back on the road, Hillary said she'd hoped to see Coole Park's famous autograph tree. "I've read that Lady Gregory had writers carve their initials into the tree trunk when they visited and hatched up plans for a literary revival." Hillary felt her throat tighten against talking about what she'd longed to see under such different circumstances on this trip. She fell silent.

Seamus drove about ten minutes through the green woodlands before he turned onto a packed dirt driveway. In less than a minute, Hillary could see a flat low bridge leading to the square stone tower, straight ahead.

"There it is, Maaa!" Claire shrieked. "A Rapunzel castle!"

Seamus pointed to the tower. "Yeats fell in love with

this place and bought it in 1917 for 35 pounds. What would it bring today—hard to imagine."

Hillary could practically see his solicitor's real estate mind in high gear. How could he be so cool? She wondered if he'd really loved Bridget.

"Of course now it's a National Heritage Site. As it should be." He parked the Yaris across the road from the tower, not far from two men working on a wooden picnic table turned on its side in a little clearing. They stood and looked over at the car.

"Sorry, mates, the tower's not open. Flood damage, ya know," yelled the older of the pair. Slim and wiry, they looked almost identical except for his short white hair in a tonsure cut. The other one had coppery curls a few shades brighter than Hillary's.

"Sean, don't you know me? It's Seamus, Bridget's fellow."

The older man limped closer to the car and peered in at the four of them. "Nope. Did'na recognize ye with that pack of folks ye've got there. What can I do for ya?"

"Need to talk to you both. Is there somewhere we can sit?"

"Picnic table's in pieces, you can see. Had some rot making it unsafe for the occasional visitor we get here. Folks come only to find the sign," he gestured toward a low building attached to the tower, "saying the tower's closed from flood damage. They get disappointed but like to walk around the grounds and by the stream." He nodded towards the water running under the bridge they'd driven over. "We like to have a table for them to set at anyways."

Seamus got out of the car. "Can we get into the bungalow?" He pointed to the thatched whitewashed

149

cottage that looked like an add-on to the tower.

"Well, we don't generally take anyone in . . ." Sean wiped his face with the back of his hand.

"I've brought along Hillary," Seamus said, "your cousin from America, granddaughter to your Uncle Patrick."

Hillary got out of the car and reached out to hug him but he nodded sharply and kept his arms folded across his chest. She introduced Claire and Sarah as they got out, but he stayed stiff as a board.

Seamus rolled his eyes. "We'd love to go sit inside. I'd prefer not to stand in the driveway to talk."

Sean said, "We're not much for talkin, but . . ." He reached into his trouser pocket and pulled out a key ring. "Come on, then."

The forest green cottage door swung open easily, and Sean motioned them in. "I've brung Bridget here to see the damage a few times." He pulled a chair out from a plank table and sat down. "We've got to get funding to fix it up proper. Love the way that gal respects the old ways."

Hillary nodded and smiled at the man who seemed to be warming up to them. The younger Sean said nothing. He stood by a dark archway that looked to Hillary like an entrance to the tower itself.

Seamus seated himself in a chair and Hillary, Claire and Sarah sat on a bench along the other side of the table.

"Sorry can't offer a cuppa, but no fire in the stove." Sean pointed toward an old wood stove along the back wall. "Why's Bridget not with ya today?"

Seamus looked at Hillary. "Well . . ." he said. His eyes darted around the dim cottage and he fell silent.

Hillary cleared her throat. "That's the bad news we

came to tell you. She was found murdered," she paused and sighed, "out in front of her Long Walk house."

"Lord, have mercy!" Sean made the sign of the cross quickly and his son followed suit. "That girl, she was messing around with powers too big for her. Fianna kept up pestering me to warn her. Said it was too dangerous. I never took it serious."

"Your mother, Fianna?" asked Hillary.

"Nah, our sister—they had the same name." Sean looked over at the cold stove. "The two of 'em, they enjoy floating about here under the thatched roof, if ye go by their cackles. Harmless, though."

"I never heard of Fianna having a daughter," whispered Hillary.

"A long story, that," said Sean. "We mostly don't talk about her." He looked over at his silent son. "He can hear 'em better 'n I—he mostly listens, is how. When we're in working on flood damage bits, he can feel all of them, hear what they mean. He tells me."

"Them?" Hillary breathed.

Sarah shuddered, pushed her arms into her cardigan and pulled it close around her shoulders. Claire scooted nearer to Hillary and looked up at her with wide eyes.

"Yea," Sean went on, "this place was Yeats' summer home and he believed it was haunted by the ghost of a soldier. Kind of a friendly place for spirits, you might say. My boy's seen the soldier floating up and down the stairway inside the tower." He looked over at his son standing erect in front of the dark doorway. "Ain'tcha, Og?" The young man nodded, barely jiggling his red curls, dark in the dim light.

"But neither of us ever noticed Yeats' boy, nope. Some photographer caught him on a picture he took in the tower though. S'posed to be the ghost of Yeats' son—Michael—standing in the sitting room." Sean scooted his chair back with a screech and stood up. "Yep, boy's birthday is comin' up soon." He cackled in a thin voice. "Wonder if the old soldier might throw him a party?"

The hair on the back of Hillary's neck bristled and she pulled Claire into a hug. Seamus stood and reached his arms up in the air swaying. "A piece of cake from a soldier," he whispered and grinned.

Hillary felt as if she were watching the scene from outside herself. She gave a cold laugh at his silly way to bring them back to normality. Claire jumped up and began hopping around on the stone floor, giggling. Sarah sat with her jaw clenched.

"Okay, so can you get that old Ford of yours down to my office tomorrow? I need you two there." Seamus paused and wiped his brow with the back of his hand. "For reading Bridget's will."

"We'll be there, sure," Sean said as he motioned for them to go ahead out the cottage door. "We lost a good one with that girl, but might be her ghost shows up here one of these days. Joins in the craic." He hooted and waved his gnarly fist in the air.

Ghosts, thought Hillary. So many kinds floating about here.

CHAPTER 20

LATER, AFTER HILLARY got Claire and Sarah settled for the night, she picked up a copy of the *Galway Advertiser* from the entry sideboard. She sat on her bed, the newspaper clutched in her hands like a lifesaver distraction against the shock and sorrow of the past few days. Lying back against the headboard, she paged through the paper with her reporter's eye. "The number of ads show the economy is doing well," she said. Ed grunted from his bed, flipping through notes for his San Joaquin County gangs speech.

When Hillary got to the editorial page, she found a letter to the editor from the Quinns. "Ed, our hosts are in the paper. Listen." She started reading aloud.

"A theme park in County Galway will interfere with tourists coming in healthy numbers to patronize our authentic small venues. Dermot Connolly and his ilk must stop using Irish stereotypes for financial gain." She looked over at Ed.

"Well, yeah, the Quinns don't want to lose B&B customers to the big hotel I've heard the developer wants to build—more than one, actually, with air conditioning."

153

He stood, took off his shirt. "Not a bad idea," he said, "now that global warming seems to be heating things up here, too."

Hillary went on reading aloud. "Here's another letter. 'This American developer is cannibalizing Irish culture in his theme park plans. He is an animal that feeds on flesh of its own species and needs to be stopped.' Wow. Bridget wasn't alone in her crusade." Hillary shook her head and sighed. "Wish I could have helped her." She gazed out the open window.

"You didn't know what all was going on, hon," Ed said, leaving his project to cross over and sit next to her.

"Or help find her killer, at least."

"We've only got a few more days here, Chickadee. The Garda don't really need our help on Bridget's case. I think you need to try and let it go."

Hillary sighed. "I don't see how I'm going to be able to leave, with this hanging in the air."

"You're getting too attached, Hill," Ed said. "Remember, we've got a life in California. Claire has to start back to school. I've got my new gang force work." He rubbed her shoulders and neck in small circles. "Remember this is our honeymoon, too." He kissed her on the inside of her wrist.

Her shoulders slumped. How could he not know how much this meant to her? But it was supposed to have been a honeymoon. She put down the paper and stood to draw the curtains closed. Suddenly his phone rang out its "Sons of Anarchy" theme song and he reached to take the call.

She got up and took a cool shower in the tiny enclosure. Afterward, she pulled one of the skimpy Quinn B&B towels tight around her, tucking in a corner over her left breast, feeling her heart pounding under her palm. She reclined on her bed, positioning herself like one of the voluptuous women lying around on chaise lounges in a Rubens' painting. She loved it when Ed compared her to them. She watched as he paced with a deep frown, knitting his eyebrows so close together they looked like a dark unibrow. His cell phone pressed tight to his ear, his voice rose with each of his words.

"Damn, Mick," he said.

He must be talking with Mickey, she thought, his buddy on the Garda force, the only one who seemed to welcome Ed's input.

After a few more seconds, Ed thrust his phone out in front of him and jabbed at the end call button. "They've got anonymous calls about ghosts on the Long Walk and feel insulted people consider them as superstitious louts." He snorted. "Mick said they found a sort of collage in Bridget's hand, pasted together from newspaper and magazines, blaming the ghost on the Long Walk. I'm supposed to be a detective, but there's nothing I can do to help."

Hillary stood, holding her towel in place with one hand, and bent down to reach with the other and fling aside Ed's duvet. She patted the white sheet.

"Come here, love. It's going to be all right, like you always tell me."

Ed ran his fingers through his damp hair, a dark auburn nearly black due to sweat from the heat, shook his head, and grinned. "I'm all sweaty."

"I need your hot body next to me," she said.

"You win, Ms. Hilly." He lay down, set his cell phone on the nightstand and forgot about it for a while.

Later Hillary moved to her bed. She knew she need-ed to bring up the subject of staying longer, there was no use avoiding it. "Except for this horrible thing," she said before she choked up.

Ed stared at the ceiling and gave her time to recover.

She shook her head hard. "The honeymoon part's been good." She wriggled her shoulders against her sheet. "Except for these twin beds! No wonder the Irish have such a low birthrate."

She leaned over and stretched her arm out across the empty space between the beds to fondle his chin, rough with its five o'clock shadow. "Next time, we'll go to Wales, I promise. Find your Kiffin family."

He smiled. "Wonder if the Welsh are smokers," he said. "These are the times I miss my little cigars." He rubbed his chin against her stroking fingers. "Being married to you has helped me forget 'em, most of the time."

Hillary felt queasy at the mention of cigar smoke, but she tried to ignore it. "I want to find out what happened to Bridget. And why." She pulled her hand away and sat up at the edge of her bed. "You're going to need to get back for the closing sessions of your conference." She rubbed the back of her neck, pursed her lips and stared at him.

He closed his eyes and sighed. "Dammit. I don't want to leave you here with a killer on the loose, Hilly. You know that."

"I'm strong. You've seen how I can take down guys twice my size, big as I am, too."

"But this killer doesn't use simple strength. He uses stealth and old ghost stories. He's crazy or wants people to think so."

"Those stories don't fool me, Ed. I can see underneath them, don't you worry."

Ed sighed. "I know you're going to do what you

want, no matter what I say." He turned away.

She sat and stared at his back, spotted with freckles in a pattern she knew by heart, wishing he could understand how important this was to her. "It's not just Bridget. I don't feel I've connected with Grandad and his life, his sister Fianna, my people." She listened for Ed's reply, but all she could hear were the soft rumbles of his snoring.

CHAPTER 21

GALWAY, IRELAND

HILLARY DROVE the few blocks to Seamus's office and parked on the street. She sat in the rental and picked at the seams of the steering wheel. "I feel nervous."

Ed lifted her fingers off and cupped her hand in his palms. "When Hanrahan reads the will, you might find out more about Bridget and that could help find her killer."

His Claddagh ring gleamed, raising Hillary's spirits for a moment until he continued. "The guys down at the Garda want us to tell them if we learn anything. So far, they've got nothing except asphyxiation, even after the preliminary autopsy."

Hillary sighed. "I should have come over sooner. I didn't even get to see her." Her eyes brimmed with tears. "Face to face. Alive." Tears spilled down her cheeks.

"Come on, Chickadee. Sitting out in the car won't get us anywhere."

Hillary pulled herself together and they took the stairs up to the law office. A receptionist led them into a conference room where Sean Mor and Sean Og were seated, looking oddly comfortable.

A woman poured water into glasses at each place at the dark wooden conference table. "Have a seat, please. My name's Aileen."

Seamus came in, adjusting his black knit tie as he strode to the conference table. "Morning, folks." He glanced over at Aileen as she set down the pitcher of water on a sideboard and adjusted stacks of papers.

He stood at the head of the table. "Any questions before we get started?" Hillary sat silent like the others.

"So, let's begin." He took a stack of paper from the sideboard and nodded to Aileen to pass out the others. She did so, leaving a thick brown envelope remaining on the sideboard. He gestured at the envelope. "We'll get to that later," he said. "First some preliminaries."

"Bridget had engaged me as executor of her estate. It will take time to move through the process, but I wanted to gather you, get things moving." He sighed. "She didn't want a funeral service as she was not devout and had no relatives nor many friends, other than the folks she worked with promoting the Irish economy."

Hillary felt empty at his words and wished she'd been here in person with Bridget instead of all that Skyping, wished she'd come over years before.

"The investigation . . ." Seamus cleared his throat, "may take some time. She wanted to be cremated and her ashes. . ." he paused, shook his head and swallowed, "scattered in front of her country house."

A wave of nausea rolled through Hillary as she couldn't help picturing Bridget's ashes. She tried to focus on the cool voice of Seamus as he talked on.

"She didn't want a service, but I want to say a few

words." He glanced around the table. Everyone sat without expression. He continued. "Bridget was an only child and her father was a leader in housing developments in the US after the Second World War. I admired him as part of a group aiming to build a global economy, and he was one of the original members of the Trilateral Commission."

Hillary felt a buzz of a shock. She hadn't realized Bridget was connected to such high level operators.

Seamus continued. "After her parents were killed, Bridget inherited the estate but didn't care about running her father's corporations, so she sold them. It left her a wealthy woman, but you would never have known, she was so down-to-earth." He smoothed back a stray curl that had fallen across his forehead and reached to brush a tear off his cheek. "I wouldn't have known about her finances, had she not chosen me as her legal representative."

He looked at the others seated motionless at the table. "You can imagine, I expect, that her wealth put a crimp in our relationship, which started as a simple business friendship. We Irish don't like to jump into marriage quickly—suppose you've heard?" He glanced at Ed.

Ed's eyes danced with good humor. "The Welsh have that reputation, too, but I didn't let it stop me." He gave Hillary's hand a squeeze.

"Well, I was already moving slow, but when I learnt of her inheritance, it stopped me in my romantic tracks." Seamus sighed. "It shouldna made a difference but truth was, it did."

His shoulders slumped. Hillary couldn't tell if she was hurting more for his grief or for her own. Everyone sat silent as he pulled out a white handkerchief from his breast pocket, took off his reading glasses and wiped each lens with care. "Now what we have left of her desire is in these pages." He touched the stack of papers in front of him. "And in that envelope." He turned and nodded at the brown packet. "A year ago, she showed me that envelope with a string loop fastener, kind of old fashioned. She was like that. Valued the traditional. She kept it on her desk out at the country house, told me if anything ever happened to her, she wanted me to get the envelope and turn it over . . ." He turned to Hillary. "To you, Hillary Broome Kiffin."

Hillary gasped. "She never mentioned it." Her heart thudded in her temples.

"So," Seamus continued, "I'll read the will and then hand over the envelope as Bridget directed." He brushed his hand over the cover sheet of the legal pages in front of him. "The Last Will and Testament of Bridget Louise Murphy."

Hillary glanced down at the cover sheet: The Last Will. She felt like she was choking. Last. Will. I will not see Bridget again. Never. Never again. Bile rose in her throat and she took small sips of cold water.

Seamus began reading aloud, naming page and paragraph numbers as he continued, tracing the text with his index finger. Hillary hardly heard a word he said.

Finally, he set down the sheaf of papers. "Bottom line, Bridget left half her estate to the Galway Housing Project, a quarter to Sean and his son . . ." he gave a sharp nod in their direction ". . . and a quarter of it to you, Hillary." He looked at her and raised his eyebrows.

She sat wide-eyed, slack-jawed and speechless.

"In addition, she left the envelope to you, Hillary. She kept me apprised of it every time I was out at her country place. She kept it front and center on her desk.

She was looking forward to sharing her research with you."

The room tightened with silence. Aileen cleared her throat. "Can I get anyone more water?" She stood and held up the glass pitcher from a tray on the sideboard.

"Watch you don't spill on the envelope!" Seamus stood and took the fat brown package in his hands. "We can move on to this now, unless anyone has questions?"

Hillary sat, stunned. How much money had he said? It was in euros, she recalled.

"Go ahead," Ed said. "We can ask questions after."

"So," Seamus said, "The contents of this envelope belong to you, Hillary. I've never seen inside it myself."

He handed the thick packet to Hillary and turned to Aileen. "Please make a note that I've turned the envelope over to the beneficiary," he said.

"The money transfers will occur after probate is complete, but I'll try to light a fire under the bankers. We'll need your bank numbers." He loosened his tie, stood and walked over to the window, pulling aside the sheer curtain and looking out on the street scene. "I can see her pulling up in her little red Audi. She loved tooling around town in it, brave heart that she was. A black soul took her from us."

He turned back to Hillary and Ed. "I've made it my passion to find that killer and get a conviction. I wish we still had capital punishment!"

Hillary felt her arms moving of their own volition. She didn't know if she wanted to learn what was in the packet or not. But of course it couldn't be helped and here with the lawyer on this big smooth wooden surface was better than ... where? Not back at the Quinns. There was no good place there, not on the little tables always set for the next meal. Not in their room, with a tiny night stand between the small beds.

No, her hands moved on their own accord, her mind in shock. All eyes in the room were on her. All except Seamus's. He remained turned away, staring out the window.

She unwound the string holding the flap closed and watched it pop open from the pressure of the thick wad inside.

Tilting the envelope, she let the papers emerge a couple inches, then clamped her fingers around the chunk, a good two inches thick. Bridget would have needed a bigger envelope soon. Or store some of it elsewhere. Where else did she keep her secrets?

Hillary looked up at Ed, then over to the Seans. No one said a word. Seamus turned away from the window, folded his arms across his chest and stared at her.

She slid the stack of papers all the way out onto the table top. They rested in a jumbled stack, some pages smaller than others, not all white, giving it the look of laundry just taken from a dryer and hurriedly folded into an unstable stack.

Some pages were legal-sized and others letter-sized. Some pages were folded sheets of newspaper. Others looked like colorful advertising flyers and some were paper hats and fans and the like.

The topmost page was crammed with handwriting in a tidy script. "That's Bridget's writing," said Seamus, nodding at the stack.

Hillary lifted the top sheet and stared at it. It was dated July 4, 2014.

Just last month.

" 'Dear Hillary,' " she read aloud. " 'I hope it is you reading this and that you got here safely. If you are

163

reading this now, it means the worst. ...' " Hillary's throat felt drier than on a hot day harvesting grapes in the vineyard. She took a swallow of water and looked around the table. The two Seans were watching her with wide eyes. She drained the water from her glass before she carried on. " '. . . has happened.' " Hillary shook her head and looked at Ed. "She knew. She knew. Why didn't she warn me?"

Hillary turned to Seamus. "Did she tell you things weren't right?"

He shook his head, frowned and cleared his throat. "She acted like nothing to worry about. Only insisted I make sure you got the envelope straight away in case anything happened. I grilled her about that since she'd taken to setting out that envelope over the past six months or so, but she wouldn't say more." He dragged his hands over his head, disturbing his black curls, and slid his palms back and forth against each other. He rubbed a hand over his mouth and left it clamped on his chin. Hillary wondered what their relationship had really been.

She turned to Sean Mor. "Were you in touch with her?"

He hung his head and mumbled. "She came up to Coole a couple times. Found us at the caretaker's cottage. Asked about the Tower ghost, you know the photographs of Yeats' son showing up all unaccounted for like that." He looked up at Hillary. "We keep all that under lock and key. Don't want the press to get hold of it, don'cha know?"

Hillary stared at him. He stayed quiet in the silence of the room. She didn't know what to ask and turned her gaze back to Bridget's letter atop the stack of papers. As if hypnotized, she continued reading aloud.

" 'The threats didn't come in the form of language. But out in front, little ghosts from wrappings around my *Times* seemed like bizarre warnings.' " Hillary's stomach did flip flops—she'd seen one over Skype. She looked up at Seamus. "She never talked about these?"

He blinked fast. "She asked me if I'd heard of ghosts around here, and sure, I knew of 'em like we all did, but that was back in June or July, when ghost fever rises around town. Ladies start hiking along the Long Walk when the weather gets good. Some for the thrill of it. She did it, too. Fearless, she was." He paced in a tight oval in front of the window. "I saw one of those tiny dolls myself last week, drove me daft." He shook his head. "But not her, too much the fighter, she was."

Hillary turned to Sean Mor. "What did she say when she was asking about Yeats' boy's ghost? What time of the year was that? Did you show her the photos?" Hillary felt a surge of energy flood her limbs, now she had something to focus on—phantoms—threats using ghosts.

Sean stayed silent, fiddling with the rim of his water glass. His son scooted his chair back and spoke up. "Da, tell the lady what happened. This is serious. This is murder."

"Ya haveta come back to Coole. I canna tell ya about it. Ya have ta see it, be there to feel it." Sean pushed his chair back. "Come on, Seanie boy, enough for one day." He nodded in the direction of the door. Father and son walked out of the room.

Hillary looked down at Bridget's letter and reread the part she'd just covered. She raised her head and looked at Seamus. "You did nothing about these ghost dolls?"

He gasped and collapsed onto a straight back chair

by the window, clutched one knee and began jiggling his leg, saying nothing.

Hillary kept reading. " 'At first I thought they might be a joke, one of the neighborhood kids being crazy around the time of year when the White Lady starts to be seen on the Long Walk.' "

"The Long Walk," Hillary whispered. "Where we found her."

She grimaced and swallowed a few times before she continued reading. " 'I just tossed the first one into a pillowcase and stuck it in the wash room cupboard. But they kept showing up on days when the *Times* ran articles about economic recovery, stories trashing the ghost estates and efforts to develop commercial projects.' "

Hillary put the letter down and rubbed her face. "I can't believe she went through all of this and didn't ask for help."

"Thick headed, she was," said Seamus. He took out his wallet, lifted a photo out and handed it over to Hillary. "You can see by the set of her jaw, she was a determined one. Did things her way. Wouldn't listen."

Hillary studied the black and white image of this friend she had met in the flesh only once, so long ago. And would never see again. She looked different in this picture from the lively woman she'd Skyped with. A perfect oval face framed by long black hair, a slim mouth in a Mona Lisa smile, dark eyes partly obscured by rimless glasses, plenty of eye makeup. Hillary couldn't see a square jaw. Now she would never see her alive. Never. She thought she was going to throw up.

"I can't keep on," Hillary said through clenched teeth. She looked at Ed. "Let's take this back to the room. Go find Sarah and Claire." She sat motionless.

Ed clamped his fingers around the stack of papers,

166

jiggled them to line up and slid them into the gaping envelope. He put the thick packet under one arm and reached down to cup Hillary's elbow. She didn't move.

"Come on, Chickadee," he said.

Hillary felt a surge of gratitude for her husband's kindness. "I hope no one knows we've got this." She gazed deep into Ed's eyes. "We don't want Sarah and Claire in danger."

"Trust me. I'll be on constant watch," Ed said, "and in touch with my Garda contacts."

"I'm ready." Hillary stood. "Make sure you have Seamus's number in your cell."

"Roger," said Ed. "I hear you." He laughed, but she shuddered and thought of their friend Roger, back home in California. Safe, home safe. When would they get back home safe?

CHAPTER 22

GALWAY, IRELAND

BACK AT THE B&B, Hillary slid the brown packet onto the top shelf of the antique armoire in their room. "I'm not sure how safe this is, but can't see anyone getting into our room, much less into this old lady." She patted the front of the chevron-design door panel.

"The Quinns keep close watch on the entry, so it should be all right," Ed said.

Hillary glanced at the windows opening onto the front parking spaces. "I kind of wish we were more in back or on the second floor," she said. "But that guy smoking out front a few days ago has checked out, so . . ." She lay down on her bed near the window. "I'll just shut my eyes for a couple minutes."

A half hour later, she woke at the sound of Ed turning the key in the door.

"All set," he said, waving a metal badge around in the air. "Garda checked my background, and my partner back home verified for me, so now . . ." he smiled and fastened the badge onto his shirt pocket, "I'm an honorary Irish policeman!"

Hillary rubbed her eyes and sat up. "Wow. That's great news."

"Got to see to the safety of my girls," Ed sat down beside her. "Now let's go find out what kind of trouble Miss Claire might have got herself into."

Hillary laughed. "Rescue Sarah, you mean."

They drove to Eyre Square and wandered around but no Sarah and Claire. "Should have made sure to give Sarah a cell of her own." Hillary raised her tank top a bit and waggled it around. "This heat is so humid here! They must have gone into the mall."

She led the way into a labyrinthine series of shops and stopped to read the sign indicating Eyre Square Centre was built in the height of the country's prosperous 1990s. Most of the shops were still tenanted, she was happy to see. The food smelled good but she was anxious to find Claire and Sarah—she couldn't help worrying about them and felt guilty about being gone so long today. They walked on down the wide hallways, eyes searching through glass-fronted shops of all sorts.

It seemed they'd covered the whole mall at least once and were retracing their steps when through the window at Flanagan's Footwear, Hillary spotted Claire, sitting like a princess in a high-rise seat with her right foot slipping into a sparkly pink trainer, the silver laces dangling at the sides. Sarah was in the seat next to her. A scrawny old man was kneeling in front of Claire, holding the shoe for her.

"Cool it," she said to Ed as he took a giant step toward the entrance. "Just act like you weren't concerned something bad had happened. Act like this is another fun day on vacation."

He worked his jaw before he nodded.

"You try and I will, too." Hillary held out her hand

for him to take it. Hand in hand, they sauntered into the store.

"Adorable," Hillary said, sitting down on the other side of Claire and nodding at the shoes.

"We were so hot outside," said Sarah, fanning herself with her Guinness dark lady fan.

"One of those little battery operated fans that have a spray mister attached might work better," said Hillary, smoothing back a few damp white hairs framing Sarah's face. "We'll get you one, and Claire, too."

The clerk tied the laces for Claire, and she walked around in front of the floor mirror for a few seconds before she turned to her father. "These are re-al-ly comforble, too, Daddy!" Hillary appreciated that she made the word "really" into three syllables to emphasize her desire but even more that she mispronounced "comfortable" since it was the only word Hillary'd ever heard her daughter mispronounce.

Ed looked at Hillary, who nodded. "Okay, sweets, let's get them if you're sure these are what you want for a Galway souvenir."

"They'll be fun for dress-up day when school starts. Can I wear them now?"

Ed nodded and paid for the purchase. The four of them walked out of the shop and agreed to a snack of soft serve ice cream. On the way to the food wagon, they passed a liquor store window that featured a bottle of Writers Tears as part of the Irish Whiskey display. Ed looked at Hillary. "We can come back later and get some."

They ordered a basket of French fries to share and a soft serve cone for each of them. Taking the snacks outside into the humid Galway afternoon, they found an empty bench in Eyre Square. Hillary worried she might not have emphasized enough to Claire to be careful about strangers. Before she bit into her vanilla cone, she reached over and rubbed Claire's shoulders. "Honey, that was a nice man back in the shoe shop, and you were with Sarah, so no problem." She patted Claire's back. "But you know that some people might act friendly to children but have bad things in mind, right?"

"I know that, Maaa." Claire picked up one of the French fries, the same the whole world over, and dunked it into a pool of bright red catsup. "I stay right with Sarah or you or Daddy." She licked the catsup off the floppy fry. "Or Mr. Hanrahan," she added.

Hillary wrinkled her face into a silly squinch to make Claire laugh. "That's it. No one goes out alone."

They sat licking their ice cream and watching the colorful tribal flags flapping in the breeze, each emblazoned with the family name of one of the city's founding families. Suddenly the last of Claire's chocolate soft serve dripped onto one of her new pink shoes.

"Maaa!" she wailed, holding her foot straight out in front of her. "I should have gotten strawberry!"

From her purse, Sarah pulled out a plastic sandwich bag and handed it to Hillary, who recognized the wet cloth inside and smiled with gratitude. "I'm prepared for accidents," said Sarah, with a wink. She tapped her purse.

Hillary scooted away from her daughter and patted the empty space she'd left between them. Claire turned and set her soiled shoe on the bench. "I hope it works. It better work!" Tears welled in her gray eyes.

Hillary set to scrubbing with the damp cloth and got

171

the soft serve wiped up, but there was a pale tan stain left on the shoe. Claire stared at it with big eyes.

"We'll work on it more when we get back," Hillary said. "Soon it'll be just a faint memory of this fun day in Galway." Fun day, indeed, Hillary thought. This was a brief break in dealing with Bridget's thick packet of papers—she had to get back to it soon.

"It's getting late." Hillary stood and Ed and Sarah followed suit. They'd bought tickets for Sarah and Claire to see a performance of Irish step dancing that showcased local talent getting ready for a national competition. Claire jumped up from the bench, shoe crisis behind her. As she skipped along the walkway, she kept her head turned to the side, looking for four-leaf clovers among bright flowers planted in concrete boxes. Hillary wished she would find even one, just one would be such a treat. But the chances of that were supposed to be one in ten thousand. Still it could be a sign things were going to turn out all right.

Ed and Hillary dropped Sarah and Claire off at the theater, and drove back to the B&B. Hillary had the odd feeling that she was headed home. There was something about the land, the air, the sky, something that sang along inside her. A humming she felt, like that in the earthy vineyard back in California. Maybe it was the soil here? A cellular thing? DNA? She felt welcome here.

But there was no Bridget to greet her except in the pages waiting. Hillary drove with heavy arms and a lump in the pit of her stomach. A mix of sorrow and fear for what she might discover in the packet at the B&B. Was there any turning back now?

She steered through the twilight. "At least I'm better now at driving on the wrong side of the road after dark," she said. Ed nodded.

Seconds later she slammed on her brakes as a teen-aged boy darted in front of the car, chasing a soccer ball.

"Hey!" Ed yelled out the window. "Watch where you're going!"

Hillary pulled off to the side. "Shit," she hissed, wild-eyed. "You drive."

She threw the car into neutral, jerked up the parking brake and got out to stand motionless on the sidewalk as Ed came round and embraced her. She slumped against his chest for a few seconds before she straightened and made her way around to the passenger side.

Ed kept on toward the B&B but pulled over near the wooded grounds of City Hall. "Let's walk in the park a bit, Chickadee. Get some fresh air, help clear the mind." He circled around to open her door. From the corner of her eye, she saw a figure in white glide among the trees, but when she stood and looked straight on, the apparition had vanished.

"Ed," she whispered. She pointed into the thicket.

He turned and scanned the woods for a few seconds. "Left the damn flashlight in the room." He shook his head. "Rental hasn't got a searchlight. Damn. Let's head back."

She slumped in the seat, her heart pounding and her stomach churning.

CHAPTER 23

THE QUINNS WERE SHOCKED. "Most folks walk the other direction, down to the hotel, bright lights all the way. I don't want to sound like I believe in such nonsense," Liam said. "But the old stories say a ghoul wanders City Hall park, some nights." He looked at his wife.

"He doesn't want to scare you," Loretta said, wide-eyed. "But truth be told, over the years, it's been more than one victim found laid out lifeless among the trees. Day times are fine, though!" She flashed a big smile. "Can I make you a cup of tea?"

Hillary shook her head and turned to unlock the door to their room, Ed close behind. Once inside, she stood motionless as if in a trance. Ed got his flashlight from the dresser top and set it on a narrow shelf next to the door.

She watched in silence as he unlocked the armoire and lifted Bridget's brown envelope out to set it in the middle of her bed. "Madame," he said, making a formal bow and waving in the direction of the bulging packet.

Hillary walked slowly between their beds, past the

174

envelope on the white duvet. Her feet felt as if she wore shoes of concrete. This was so odd, this reticence. Always before, she was one to jump in and read anything, even sneaking a peek at a stranger's eBook on an airplane.

But this letter. It was so different. Bridget's last words. Guilt weighed on Hillary's shoulders like a lead cape. She should have gotten to Bridget sooner. While she had a chance to help. Hillary flashed on that morning so long ago when she woke to find her mother gone. The chant from that old childhood game—now poor "somebody's" dead and gone, dead and gone, dead and gone—echoed through her memory. Was her mother leaving partly her fault, too?

Hillary gave her head a couple hard shakes and turned to sit near her pillow. "Let's get on with it." She opened the packet and fingered out the top sheet, the letter to her from Bridget. Letters. For years she'd yearned for even one from her mother. How would she feel if she ever got a letter from her mother? She looked up at Ed. "I need a drink."

"We'll walk down to that liquor store after you get through." He sat across from her on his bed.

Sighing, she glanced at Bridget's handwriting. "She was precise, careful, you can tell from her writing. It's so tiny and square. Like a draftsman's."

Ed nodded. "Keep going."

She turned the onionskin paper over. "Black ink on both sides. Kind of hard to make out with shadows from the backside."

"Want me to read it?" He stood and sat on the other side of the packet. It lay between them, framed by their bodies.

"It's so hot in here." She laid the letter down and

clawed her fingers through her loose hair, lifted it into a thick bunch and let it go. She bent, pulled open the nightstand drawer and grabbed a tortoise shell hair clip. She wound her hair into a thick twist, then clamped the clip over it all. "There." She wiped her forehead with the back of her hand and looked at Ed. "Can you open the window, let in some air?"

He slid aside the white curtains and cranked open the two panels that flanked the bay window fronting the B&B. "Can't put off finishing it much longer, babe." He nodded in the direction of the packet. "It's getting late. We have to pick up Sarah and Claire in an hour."

Hillary lifted the letter and held it in the flat of her palm. Straightening her spine, she traced a finger half way down the page and read aloud in a firm voice, " 'The ghost dolls were strange . . .' " Hillary wrinkled her nose as she spoke Bridget's words from the page. " 'But as each one showed up by the newspaper, they began to feel like a tiny family. I was an only child.' "

Hillary looked at Ed. "An only child. Just like me." Tears welled and she slumped her shoulders, the letter clutched in her hand. "And Claire, too. Wish they'd been able to meet," she muttered.

Ed moved the packet back and sat hip to hip with her, reaching his arm around her shoulder.

"It'll be all right." He rubbed her neck with his thumb, in little circles the way she liked. She closed her eyes and rolled her head side to side as he massaged her neck and shoulders.

After a long minute, she straightened and stood, letter in hand. Edging past Ed's knees, she walked to the middle of the room and turned to face him. "If I stand, I can get a better grip on myself." Raising the letter to read from it, she glanced toward the front window.

A shadowy figure slipped from view, off to the right.

"Ed," she breathed. "Someone's out there . . . listening," she whispered.

He jumped up, grabbing his flashlight on the way out and thumbing his cell phone. He dashed through the entry and out the front door, Hillary close behind.

His phone pressed to his ear, Ed sprinted past the parking spaces and along the sidewalk. Hillary felt glad he was calling the Garda for backup. He ran two blocks to the City Hall grounds and turned to scan the wide swath of trees, Hillary right behind him, letter still in hand.

"Oh my God," Ed said as he turned and saw her. "Did you lock the bedroom?"

She went pale as fish-belly skin, about faced and darted back the way she'd come. Ed rushed past and made it through the front door and into their room a few seconds before her.

"It's gone," he said as Hillary tailed him into the bedroom. She ran to the bed, bent and patted the empty place where they'd left the envelope. She looked at the letter in her other hand, then stared at the duvet. She felt numb.

"Around back," he snapped. "The Garda should be here soon."

He tore out into the entry, past the breakfast room and through the dark kitchen. The Quinns were nowhere in sight. He rushed out the back door and Hillary trailed him through the back gate.

She looked up and down the dimly lit alley, swirling with mist. A green trash bin stood every fifty feet or so, as if guarding the dank passageway. She stumbled and reached her hand out against the brick wall to keep from falling. The letter fell to the cobblestoned pavement and skittered in the breeze. She jerked down to clutch it tight, took a second to catch her breath and ran to catch up with Ed.

"He got away," he said, a dejected look in his eyes. It was that hound dog expression she hated to see on his lean face whenever the topic of unsolved cases came up. The look of failure.

Bile rose in Hillary's throat. She swallowed several times and studied the crushed letter, the ink blurring into smudges where her fingers gripped it. "Holy Mary," she whispered. She opened her hand and stared at the letter, stuck to her sweaty palm.

"We could search the park." Ed nodded in that direction, "but it's too late. He got away with it." He jerked his shoulders one at a time, cracking his bones. "We need help," he admitted. "But the Garda are running on Irish time. Got to report this to the Quinns. Damn. I'm sorry, Hill."

"All her papers, gone," Hillary said in a flat monotone, "and the letter . . ." She pinched it between her thumb and index finger and waved it in the air. "It's all smeary." They stared at each other.

Hillary had never before felt this helpless. She closed her eyes and summoned the image of her father chasing a story under the pressure of a deadline, focused and fierce. She stiffened and stood erect, clenched her jaw and led the way back through the dark kitchen. In the entry, she pushed the buzzer calling the Quinns from their upstairs quarters before she returned to their room.

She stared at the empty spot on her bed where the packet had been. A fuchsia print pillowcase near the headboard seemed to mock her with its rosy frivolity. She placed the letter in the armoire and lifted the small skeleton key from the hook inside. She locked the wardrobe door and pushed the key deep inside her bra. "At least we have Bridget's letter. Got to let it dry out." She looked at Ed. "Don't let anyone have it."

"It could be considered evidence," he said through tight lips.

"It's my personal property." She glared at him.

The waa waa of Irish sirens grew closer, and Hillary was relieved to see a Garda car pull into a parking space in front. Two young officers nearly crashed into the Quinns as the four of them convened in the B&B entry.

Hillary beckoned them all into the room. "It's late," she said to Ed. "You stay here and tell them what happened. I'll go get Sarah and Claire." Hillary drove off, alone with her thoughts. On the way back from the theater, she took care driving through the mist and half-listened to Sarah and Claire rhapsodize about the step dance show. But she barely heard a word, her mind swirling with worries.

The Garda officers—both so young she could picture them in school uniforms—were still there when Hillary got back. Ed took Sarah and Claire upstairs to their room, so Hillary could give her version of the theft to the officers. The Quinns stood to the side, taking it all in.

"Yes," Hillary said, "we thought about chasing him down to City Hall park, but it's foggy and so laced with trees, he would have already slipped away."

"How do ya know about the trees?"

"On our walks, sometimes we see a shadow moving among them, but when we stop to pay attention, the shadow never materializes."

The officers exchanged glances. "We don't want you poking around down there."

"Why not?"

"Let's just say the old stories have been known to give cover for folks up to no good."

"Cover?"

"You never heard of the ghosts of Galway?"

Hillary was shocked at their attitude. "You don't believe in ghosts?"

"Nah, but Fáilte tries to keep tourists away from certain places, that park bein' one of 'em."

"Amazing," she said, feeling too exhausted to say one more word.

"Call us if you're in trouble again," said the younger cop. He handed her his business card. "Put the number in your phone contacts."

Liam Quinn double-checked their narrow front windows and showed them how to fasten them open just a few inches. Hillary knew someone lurking could still hear them, but at least they let a breath of air in to the west-facing room.

"Think I might buy one of those electric fans, this heat keeps up," Liam said.

"One?" Loretta frowned at him.

"Can't afford to outfit the whole place." He looked at Hillary and Ed. "The woman's too loose with a penny. Got to watch her. You see how she outfitted the breakfast room all fancy." They walked out, arguing how to budget their euros.

Ed sat up against his headboard, legs straight and crossed at the ankles. He pulled his new tin whistle out from his pocket and tapped it against his open palm. "Had one of these when I was a kid. We called it a pennywhistle and thought it was for Welsh tunes." He blew on it softly. "Wonderful to find 'em in shops here."

Hillary unlocked the armoire, relieved to see the ink had dried. She carried the letter over to the bed.

"Want me to read it?" Ed mouthed the whistle and breathed softly into it.

Hillary sighed. "Got to finish it tonight." Pulling her hair clip off, she combed her fingers through her hair and reclipped it before she started in. She mumbled through a review, slowing down to articulate important spots, her voice firm.

" '. . . dolls . . . rubber bands . . . *Irish Times* . . . only child.' " She sighed, set the letter aside and yanked open the nightstand drawer to pull out a box of liquor-filled chocolates.

She lifted the lid and held out the box to Ed. "Since it's too late to go get a drink," she said.

He thrust out his hand palm up to reject the candy. She unwrapped a chocolate and put it in her mouth. She couldn't imagine feeling this nervous if she got a letter from her mother. Not that that would ever happen. She licked her fingers one at a time, then wiped them hard against her pants leg.

She read Bridget's words in a calm and throaty voice. " 'When I came over in '05, I was on a task for my father's company, same as your grandfather's Broome Construction but on America's east coast. After Ireland's economy came tumbling down, he wanted in on the rebuilding, so he sent me to investigate because I'd done post-doctoral work in global development.' " Hillary stopped to look at Ed, who'd swapped out his whistle for a small memo pad and started taking notes.

"Wow, she never mentioned a Ph. D." She continued on with the letter.

" 'After Teddy died, I had no reason to go back to

California. I stayed on here and was asked to join some movers and shakers, billionaires and academics intent on creating a worldwide organization to profit themselves first, but people of the world, too.' "

Hillary turned the page over. "Hardly any smeared ink here." She put the letter down and opened the nightstand drawer.

Ed got himself a glass of water from the bathroom sink.

She rummaged in the box of chocolates for one filled with Bailey's Irish Cream and unwrapped it slowly, taking a few minutes to chew and swallow it before she pronounced, "That's my last chocolate tonight."

She returned to the letter. " 'At the same time, I was researching your grandfather's background. Had started that back when I was engaged to Teddy, since it would have become my family history, too, if he had lived.' "

"I knew she'd done that," Hillary said. "She sent me stuff on the Broomes."

Ed nodded and polished off his water. "Better stick with the letter, or we'll be up all night."

Hillary gave her head a quick shake and continued. " 'The group insisted no projects be built on historic land. They wanted to provide legendary sites with vistas needed to showcase them, as in the UK, instead of being crowded tight by the side of the road like Trinity College and Dublin Castle.' "

"Interesting," said Ed. "I wondered about that."

Hillary kept on. " 'That rule vexed developers like Dermot Connolly, Ryan Shanahan and Casey Bengal who were pushing the envelope, proposing huge projects like theme parks, sports stadiums, and housing developments. I've uncovered information that can obstruct their projects. Beyond historic, what I learned is tragic and if it gets out, the massive bad publicity can kill their proposals in the planning stages.' " Hillary frowned at Ed before she continued.

" 'I'll close with the password for my country house computer, where you'll find originals of most of these items in the envelope.' " Hillary raised her head. "Ed," she whispered, "it's smeared. I can't make it all out." She studied the paper. "It looks like -eddy and -20." She stared wild-eyed at Ed. "Eddy?"

He shook his head.

"Teddy?" She read the letter's last line, one word at a time. " 'Please. Carry. On. Love. Bridget.' "

Hillary set the letter down and inhaled deep, held her breath then threw her head back, flapping her lips in a soft neigh. "This is a lot more than I expected. I don't see how I can get into her computer in the few days we have left."

"Not to mention the fact that if she was killed for this—if that's what happened—you're not safe pressing on with it, either." Ed slid his notepad into his shirt pocket next to the little tin whistle. "Claire and Sarah might be in danger, as well." He took off his shirt and hung it in the armoire. "We need to leave this to the Garda, go home on schedule and hope for the best."

"God no, I can't just leave this hanging and run back to California. No," she said, watching Ed take off his shorts and disappear into the bathroom. The sound of water running soothed her nerves. She closed her eyes for a minute.

Ed came back into the bedroom, holding his toothbrush topped with striped toothpaste. Gesturing with the brush as if pointing his finger at her, he ticked off the reasons to go home and forget about exploring the issues raised in Bridget's letter.

"First, nothing you do can bring Bridget back to life, to put it bluntly. Second, this is not your country, not your problem, but most important," he waggled the toothbrush in the air, "you are responsible for Sarah and Claire!" The toothpaste bobbled and fell off the brush to land on Ed's white duvet. "Along with me," he added.

Hillary doubled over in hysterical laughter.

"It's not funny, Hill." With his brush, Ed deftly scooped up the blob of toothpaste and disappeared into the bathroom.

She held her stomach and rocked back and forth on the bed, feeling sick and nervous. If they left, she would be abandoning Bridget, who had lost her life over whatever this was really about. And it looked to be connected with her father's family. Her father, who stood by her when her mother up and ran out on them when she was just a bit older than Claire. But I can't endanger her. Or even myself and risk Claire losing her mother, too.

Hillary stood and stripped off her sweat-soaked tee then peeled off her bra. She sucked in her stomach to unbutton her shorts and let them drop to the floor. She stood rooted to the spot. Bridget would no longer be able to perform these simple tasks. Or any tasks.

She peeled off her panties, put her dirty clothes into a net bag and walked in on Ed, shaving at the sink in his boxers, printed with Guinness harps and shamrocks. He waggled his rear end up against her belly as she edged by, too hot and tired to respond. She stepped in to the shower, turned on the water and stood with her face raised up to the spray, trying to rinse her mind of worries that darted and sprang from every direction.

Without a sound, Ed slipped in behind her, sans

boxers, she could feel him. Such a Jack Spratt to her roundness, she thought. Joy flooded her belly at the comfort of their pairing and her worries ran with the water down the old shower drain.

CHAPTER 24

GALWAY, IRELAND

SEAMUS HUNG UP THE PHONE. Fecking banks always took their time to get funds distributed. It wasn't so urgent for the others, but he wanted to get Hillary's money to her before she left Ireland in a few days. Who the feck would have thought he'd have to be settling Bridget's estate, her so young and alive.

He stared at her picture, front and center on his desktop, beautiful and fresh behind glass in the frame. Here she was encased forever, like a princess in a fairy tale. Tears welled. He took off his reading glasses and rubbed his eyes with his fingertips to ease the pressure, his palms massaging his cheeks at the same time.

He got his cell out of the desk drawer and punched in Dermot's latest burner number. As usual it went to voice mail. Damn power-hungry man. Seamus pawed around in his top desk drawer for some antacids. Never needed 'em since the crash when business was about to go belly up. He was chewing a couple Rennies when the burner rang.

"Yeah," he said, crunching the last of the chalky tablets and swallowing fast.

"Solved one of your problems," said Dermot.

"What the hell do you mean?"

"Took care of that Blackwoods project."

"That was never my project. Who've you got setting up your dirty work? Some respectable mate, ya? A crooked doctor?"

Dermot let loose his horsey bray.

"A dodgy dentist?"

Another hollow hoot.

"A hinky accountant?"

Silence on the line.

That was it. He'd guessed it. Seamus hit the End button and shoved two more Rennies into his mouth. He sat and chewed over this news. An accountant, a respectable business man who could reach out to contract killers. Suddenly the memory of a nearby storefront came to mind.

He marched a couple blocks down Merchants Road to Kane Brothers Accounting. In the window stood engraved testimonials: "A professional and efficient accountancy & tax service."

He strode in, surprised at how smoke-filled it was, and glad he rarely lit up a cigar in the office. He demanded to speak to Kane.

"Which one, sir?" The receptionist looked and sounded like a well-turned out news anchor on TV. Classy lady.

"How many are there?"

"The Kane brothers are twins." She flashed a gleaming smile. "Look alike but different as night and day."

Just then a door opened and a short bald man carrying a brief case in one hand and a cigarette in the other darted into the lobby and out the door to the street.

Seamus flashed a questioning look at the receptionist.

She nodded with pride "That was Tom. Our out-and-about man. Works with contacts in the field—even overseas sometimes."

Seamus clenched his jaw.

"Would you like to make an appointment, sir?"

"What's the other's name?"

"John, sir, John and Tom Kane, they are."

Seamus turned on his heel and left. Wouldn't do any good to directly confront a sneaky bastard in the business of murder for hire.

CHAPTER 25

HILLARY SAT FEELING DAZED at the table she'd come to think of as theirs. She'd been too numb for bad dreams even—one thing to be grateful for. Ed was on the phone with a Garda detective and was staying in town to help work the case instead of going on the bus tour with them. She felt hollow inside like the only thing she had energy for was to sit staring out the window in a stupor. But she'd put down a non-refundable deposit back in the spring when she had no clue things would turn out like this. Claire and Sarah would love it, though, and it might take her own mind off the horror of finding Bridget.

Hillary blew on her steaming cup of coffee and stared out the bay window at cars in the front lot. Who was that shadow of a man loitering last night? Had he taken the packet? Why? Where was it now?

Her veins felt like cold lines drawn under the skin of her arms, heavy as if blood was parked inside her. Her stomach was empty and growling but the thought of food sounded impossible. She stared at Ed's buttered hunk of soda bread with apricot chutney on the side

189

and had to swallow three or four times to suppress her nausea.

Claire and Sarah burst into the room, Claire's hair braided up in two plaits and crisscrossed over the top into a crown. She walked around the room and waved like a royal figure sauntering along a street in Disneyland.

"You look lovely, Princess," Hillary said. She cleared her throat. "Guess where we're supposed to go this morning?"

"To a castle?" Claire shrieked, dropping her poised stance.

Sarah's brown eyes danced behind her red-framed glasses. She'd put her long white hair up into two braids, a version of what she'd done with Claire's. "We're off to see the wizard?" Sarah sang out.

"Nope." Hillary couldn't help laughing. "We already saw Ballylee and the wizard's in the Oz movie, hiding behind curtains. Today we're off to hunt for Irish ghosts."

Claire squealed with joy and bounced over to get a bowl of Cheerios. Hillary knew she should get something to eat, even just a yogurt, forget all the sausage and fried eggs and potatoes, but nothing on the sideboard looked appealing. It was going to be a long trip with an overnight stay at an old house in Connemara.

Hillary had invited Loretta along in Ed's place, knowing she made it a practice to do tourist things, so she could better advise guests, and felt comfortable leaving Liam in charge. A few minutes before nine, the tour bus pulled into the front lot, sporting Ghosts of Galway signs on the sides.

On the way out, Claire spotted a pack of teenagers

bicycling down the street. They wore green tee shirts imprinted with "Cross Country Riders" in white block letters.

"Look!" Claire waved and several of the bicyclists waved back, laughing. "I hope they don't get stuck in bogs like in *Bike Tour Mystery*." Claire looked at Hillary. "But that was just pretend, right Maaa?"

Hillary smiled at her daughter's bright mind. "Yes, Princess, fiction—make believe, not real." Claire was going through three or four books a week from the Lodi library back home. Old enough to read beyond her age group, yet young enough to listen as Ed read aloud to her.

"That's what I mean, Mrs. Quinn," Claire nodded firmly at Loretta. "Fiction."

The four of them climbed in and took up most of the back row in the bus. "Have you heard of Nancy Drew?" Hillary asked Loretta, who shook her head no.

"She solves crimes in mysteries for young readers," Hillary said. "Mostly in the U.S., but Claire here," she fingered one of her daughter's blond braids interlaced with thin pink and green ribbons, "young as she is, loves them. She read one that took place near here," Hillary explained. "And the young people in the book get trapped in a bog trying to chase down some sort of killer."

Hillary rubbed the sudden gooseflesh on her arms. Some sort of killer.

Loretta leaned forward. "Our peat bogs here are not so much the kind bodies can sink down into."

Sarah nodded and continued talking about the books. "The mysteries are by Carolyn Keene," she said. "Keene. Good name for someone keen enough to get Nancy out of trouble over that long series."

Hillary's stomach growled and she wished she'd brought along a scone from the sideboard after all. "That's the name the publisher used for several authors," Hillary said. Talk about ghostwriters who had it made, she thought, a fiction of a writer. Carolyn Keene—a pen name for any writer who could convey the tone and spirit of the legendary girl detective from River Heights, another fiction. There were plenty of haunted settings in those books.

Hillary had loved reading them as a kid and connected to Nancy because she'd been raised by a strong and kind father. But what happened to Nancy's mother? That's the mystery they never revealed. She dug around in her tote bag for a Tums.

A square-jawed young man with a headful of black curls stood at the front of the bus and began talking into a microphone, smiling and nodding his head. "Welcome! Failte! My name's Sean, but you can call me Seannie."

Same as Fianna's son and grandson, thought Hillary. It was a common name here. She liked it. Claire had been a name out of nowhere, actually Scots. It just sounded so right—Claire Kiffin. She liked to call herself Claire Kitten, and had posters of kittens on her bedroom wall at home.

"Me troupers," Seannie called out. Troupers. He was like a scout leader.

"How are ye, after last night?" He laughed. "Too much of the craic?" Several passengers moaned.

"The hotel bar at the end of today's tour will be servin' plenty of 'Cure,' for your heads." He waggled the microphone and tossed it from hand to hand. "To occupy your minds, I'm going to tell stories along the

192

way, if that sounds good, ya?"

The passengers called out "okay" and "fine," a bit louder now.

He smiled and pointed his microphone at the man busy driving the bus. "Sims, me troupers. We've got Sims, the safest driver over all Ireland. Never says a word, keeps his eyes and his mind on the road. Wouldn't hurt to hand him a couple euros at the end of the trip. We'll be overnight out in Connemara, and drop you back here tomorrow. Thursday."

He explained that all children in Ireland must learn the Gaelic language and that they pronounce their English in the Irish way. "We don't say some of the sounds you see in the words, no. So it sounds to ya like I'm saying Turs-day, eh?" He laughed.

"I'll sing for ya, too—that's what I'm going for, after this tour business, ya know? A singer. Retire young to a cottage by the roadside, ya. Pick up one of our 'ghost houses,' nice and cheap now. I'll start out with a piece I wrote and get ya in the mood for our supernatural sites."

He began singing a lively tune. Claire nodded and clapped along. "Sounds like 'Lord of the Dance' music, Maaa," she said. She tapped her feet on the bus floor in time with his song, holding her arms straight down.

"We heard it last night. Too bad you missed it," said Sarah. She looked over and gave Claire a big smile. "I bet you could take step dance lessons back home."

Hillary felt torn. She knew she had to find out what happened to Bridget. But would they need to stay longer over here? Claire was about to begin second grade. Would it be fair to delay her start, put her behind her classmates? Hillary hoped Ed would find some leads as to who killed Bridget and why. Then they could fly home Sunday as scheduled. But could she leave with Bridget's ashes not yet scattered?

The bus parked at Nimmo's Pier and let them out across the inlet from the Long Walk. Hillary shuddered at the sight and looked away from where she and Loretta had discovered Bridget's body, just a few days ago. Loretta stood close to Hillary as Seannie pointed across the inlet and told of ghosts wandering near the Spanish Arch, where fisherwives sold herring and salmon in days gone by.

"Ya, locals claim it's a hotbed of hauntings. Tales of the odd spirit here and there have been told for decades. Just two years back, a local man was taking pictures here and later noticed the image of a figure wearin' a dark hooded cloak standing in one of the shots. But," Seannie rolled his eyes, "it does na appear in any of his other shots. Some say it's a 19th Century nun from Claddagh. The truth can't be known for sure," he said.

Hillary loved hearing the way Seannie left out the "th" in truth—sweet and funny, "troot." He handed around a photo showing a blurry image of a figure draped in black. It stood on a grassy open space that matched the open fields next to Claddagh Quay, the long stone and concrete structure beside the Corrib River as it runs into Galway Bay. "Plenty of hookers," he said, "and I don't mean the hookers trolling the streets of big cities." He wiggled his hips. "Na, these hookers are the boats called that for the hook method of fishing they carried on. These hookers," he gestured towards a small black painted boat with a red sail out on dry dock nearby, "they used to be tied up here and their fish unloaded for the wives to take across the bridge and sell under the Spanish Arch. The ghosts might be those who left this life with unfinished business, ya.

"One thing's for sure—whatever this ghost in the photograph is, it's made many people's midnight strolls on The Long Walk come to an end, for fear of meeting up with the phantom!" He swept his hand along the fronts of colorful townhouses rowed up along the Long Walk. "Even so," he said, his green eyes dancing, "it's been a favorite walking destination for three centuries. That promenade's immortalized in songs like 'Galway Girl.'" He burst into his own rendition of the popular song.

Later, the bus headed into the tourist section of downtown Galway where they got out and walked around to look at the Druid Lane theater where Seannie described that resident ghost. "Many of these buildings you see here were convents years back and lately people in the shops claim they've seen a nun walking down these streets, stuck between this world and the next, for God only knows what reason. Ya, and back in the '80s, the actor Sean McGinley was working in the theatre late one night when he heard strange sounds. He got out of the building instead of hangin' around to investigate." Seannie tapped Hillary on the shoulder. "Wouldn't you?"

She shuddered and looked at Sarah. They laughed in a half-hearted way.

"Time to get on our way." Seannie guided them toward the bus.

They headed along the road to Salthill and drove by a park. Loretta nodded toward a sculpture on the green near the water. "That's where the memorial to the starving children stands," she muttered. "Tucked away so most tourists never see it."

Hillary nodded. Another example of what Bridget must have wanted to bring out in the open more in her idea for a memorial inside the theme park. Hillary was glad Claire hadn't heard Loretta and they had driven quickly by the park.

The bus wound along the Wild Atlantic Way skirting the Atlantic Ocean. "We're now in Connemara National Park." Seannie looked out the bus windows and pointed at the barren landscape. "Sure ye've heard of the Irish bogs, ya? We've what we call a blanket bog here with some lovely plants happy in that rich soil."

"Bogs, Maaa!" Claire's mouth popped open. "I thought you said they weren't here?"

"That's a different kind and besides, we're not going to be near them, Princess. Our hotel's on the seacoast, not next to any bogs. Listen to Seannie."

"Ya," he was saying, "ancient mountains were scraped down to the bones by the glaciers way back, leavin' us seein' the bare grey granite. The fields are divided by low stone walls made by clearing the land so it could be planted."

Hillary's eyes traced the rolling hills, some so tall they were dubbed mountains though they were a far cry from the Sierra Nevadas she knew so well in California. They were so bright green they almost looked fake.

Seannie carried on. "If you had weeks to spend in Connemara National Park, you could hike hundreds of acres of mountain, heather and bog walks. Ye might even come across the ghost of Connemara Molly, who could see your fortune in a cuppa tea, she could."

Hillary shivered, entranced with the land she'd read

and dreamed about so long.

"But we've our own troubles to handle tonight," he said. "We're near our hotel with its grand food and comfy beds and ..." he paused and rolled his eyes. "And its own ghost stories!

"The place is where the famous have gathered, including our own Yeats. Ya know his poem where the center cannot hold?" He looked up and down the row of bus passengers. Hillary was glad to see most of them nodded at the line from Yeats' famous piece, "The Second Coming."

"Well," Seannie said, "his own center was what you call on the loose side, as well, it was. The fellow worked hard to communicate with the other world. He held a séance in the lodgings we're headed for, he did, and used automatic writing to converse with a supposed spirit. This one showed itself in a mist by the fireplace. But no sweet nun spirit this, no. This one was a boy, a pale boy with a tormented expression on his face."

Hillary looked at Claire. She sat silent and rapt as Seannie talked on.

"Yeats himself had a boy he feared would be murdered, didya know?" he looked around at the passengers. "He wrote a poem asking ghosts to guard him from harm. But at the place we're spending tonight, Yeats was known to have seen doors opening on their own, pitiful groans coming from all over the house, bed-sheets pulled from beds, and guests pulled from them also!" Seannie cackled.

"Others say these ghosts respect no one's privacy. Women have seen faces looking at them from the mirror as they undress." He stood erect and wide-eyed. "So, all of ye, cover your mirrors before you get ready for bed tonight. Make Seannie and Sims here," he backed up and patted the silent old driver on his scrawny shoulder, "make the both of us happy to see all of ye safe and well in the morning!"

Hillary ignored the goose bumps rising along her arms and legs. She reached out wide to hug Claire and Sarah and nod at Loretta. "We'll be fine. This is just for entertainment, all these spooky stories." But her reality was getting that raggedy edge she usually felt only in nightmares. She laughed at their solemn faces but she felt no joy.

CHAPTER 26

CONNEMARA, IRELAND

THE CONNEMARA HOUSE foyer was done up in shades of white and gray, with gauzy silk coverings hanging at the sides of tall glass windows that flanked the front doors. Hillary marched to the reception counter and nudged aside a framed sign as she handed her credit card to the desk clerk. Sarah picked up the sign and read it out loud. "Psychics have existed in Ireland for centuries, leftover from long ago days, full of superstition and mysticism. To talk to a fortuneteller is to have a taste of old Irish culture. Connemara House is proud to bring our guests a variety of those holding special powers from the unseen worlds. This month, we are pleased to have with us Dukker, a palm reader who studied under the esteemed Cheiro."

Sarah put the sign down. "We've come clear around the world to find a man reading wrinkles in hands like old Rough Winds studied them in leather back on the reservation," she said.

Hillary finished registering and picked up the sign. She studied the image of a black-haired man with swarthy skin and a red kerchief tied around his neck, a disembodied palm cradled his own big hand. "These people are just making good guesses, if you ask me. It's odd," she said. "This one reminds me of one of those buskers hanging around down at the city centre the other day, the look in his eyes and that black hair standing up off a widow's peak." She was skeptical and uneasy over this sort of thing. She set down the sign and led the way upstairs to their rooms.

Hillary's packet of face wipes and tube of moisturizer barely fit among the items already cluttering the white china tray on the doily-covered bureau. She unpacked a few things while Loretta took a shower. Hillary went down the hall and found Sarah powdering her nose at an oval mirror over a tall antique dressing table.

"This glass is so old, it has a sort of mirror inside a mirror effect," Sarah said. "I can see why superstitious folks might think a ghost was watching them." She laughed and looked at Hillary. "Come on, the hotel flaunts these elements to draw tourists, dearie, you know that."

Hillary nodded. "They go overboard to set up their mystique and do a good job of it. But I don't fall for that sort of thing."

Within an hour Hillary was leading the way downstairs to the dining room lighted with candles in wall sconces and on each table. A man she assumed must be the fortuneteller was gliding around the dim room. His long black hair rose up off his forehead, as if to accentuate his widow's peak and show off his swarthy complexion. Hillary felt her pulse quicken as the man approached their table.

"Madame," he nodded. "May Dukker read for you?"

An inertia suddenly possessed her. She remembered that day at the old state fair in Sacramento. Her mother had slipped inside a red and gold tent hung with a poster of a huge glass ball on the front—a white blurry shape seemed to shimmer inside the ball. A sudden summer breeze arose and rattled the poster. Hillary turned to look up at her father. His scowl delivered an unspoken message: don't go for that nonsense. "Come on, Princess. Let's go get you a corn dog." They left and went home. Hillary never thought about it back then, but how had her mother gotten home that night?

The dark-eyed man turned to kneel down in front of Claire. "Or, shall I see what's in the young girl's future?" Hillary observed the curly ponytail hanging ten inches down his back as he reached out his lined brown palm towards her daughter's hand.

"No!" Hillary jumped up and stood between the two of them. "Thank you anyway, but . . ." She felt heat flush her cheeks.

"Do my hand," called out Sarah, laughing. "We had all sorts of ways to predict what was coming, up on the reservation. I've had 'em all. Now, let's hear yours."

The man went to Sarah and took her palm. He traced his finger back and forth and in a circle, and he hummed softly as he repeated his motions. Hillary felt light-headed and forced herself to sit back down.

The man pursed his lips then began speaking. "I see tragedy ten years back," he said, looking at Sarah. She narrowed her eyes.

Of course, she looks like the typical widow, thought Hillary, that's just a good guess on his part. She gripped the menu tightly to keep from trembling.

He sighed and shook his head. "I see sadness just a

few days ago, as well." His eyes grew large and he blinked several times. "Tonight, happy times with your friends and family." He looked at the four of them circled around the table. That's nothing, thought Hillary. He can see us all sitting here.

"But," he said and clicked his tongue, his dark eyebrows forming into a black V. He brushed at Sarah's palm, then peered at it before he shot a look at Hillary. He nodded at her then at Sarah. "Enjoy the dinner but think about leaving after. I see danger tonight for you." He stared gravely at Sarah.

Sarah looked at Hillary. "This man and his fortunes must account for the high prices here," she said. "Boost up the haunted hotel flavor, for sure." She shook her head, withdrew her hand and said to him, "Go on and visit the other tables. I'm hungry and ready to order!"

A waiter appeared at Sarah's side, pad in hand. "Yes, my lady, what is your pleasure?"

"I'll have the mussels in white wine," Sarah sang out. "Like Molly Malone." She laughed.

"Maaa, I wanted my fortune told," whined Claire.

"Sometime at home, honey, maybe the Grape Festival next month." Hillary ordered the same macaroni and cheese entrée as Clair said she'd like, then excused herself to go phone Ed, and get a breath of fresh air in the foyer.

"Any news?" She stared out into the dark night through the gossamer window coverings.

"Not much," he said. "The autopsy report shows what we thought—strangulation. She's been released to the funeral home."

Hillary pressed her hot forehead lightly against the glass windows, their cool surface calming her panic. Now Bridget would be sent to be cremated. Hillary wondered if the trip could get any worse as she rang off and returned to the table.

After dinner, they sat in the parlor and sipped liqueurs while Claire played checkers with Seannie the tour bus driver. Hillary noticed he was letting Claire win and giving her a whoop of kudos before he took a seat in front of the fireplace and began to sing "Athenry," the ballad of the Irish man deported to Australia for stealing corn to feed his family.

"These lyrics are so sad," said Hillary, looking at Sarah.

"They say you're not really Irish if you don't think the world will break your heart," said Sarah. "At least that's what I read in the ladies' room." She nodded toward the hall. "It's the Irish way. Maybe makes 'em feel better?"

Loretta grimaced. "We have jolly tunes too." She called out to Seannie, "Lead us in a round of 'There's Whiskey in the Jar.' "

The music was lively but Hillary felt worn to the bone and glad the creepy fortuneteller was no longer in sight. She was ready to get to bed and sleep so the night would be over and she could get back to Galway and Bridget's computer files. Find out what she was keeping so secret. What she might have been killed for.

Hillary tucked Claire in, happy she wanted to listen to the story Hillary told about Irish fairies and leprechauns and tiny new shoes. She left the room as Sarah began telling the story about the Miwok and the Coyote stealing the shoes from the children to give them to the fish, trying to trick them into giving the roe to Coyote. Claire had a dreamy smile on her face, and her eyeslids fluttered and closed. Hillary smiled at Sarah and tiptoed out of their room down the hall to join Loretta. Time to get some rest.

A cradle made of padded white muslin rocked silently against the wallpaper, stretching inch by inch up toward the ceiling. Cries of babies vibrated the walls, babies yearning for words. The cries rose to screams and then of a sudden, fell silent.

Hillary woke from the dream feeling empty and drained. A faint light shone through the windows. Claire had slipped in beside her in the night and was fast asleep, Punzy and Beanie clutched in her arms, their legs dangling down the side of the bed. Hillary watched her by the faint gleam of a dim moonlight, loving the quiet motion of her little chest rising and falling in slow rhythm.

Loretta was snoring softly from the other bed. Hillary checked her phone. It was four o'clock. She slipped out from under the duvet and padded down the hall to check on Sarah. There was even less moonlight in this room, and she couldn't see Sarah from where she stood at the doorway. She tiptoed around to the other side of the bed and poked at the top of the bedding. Nothing.

She suddenly realized the duvet was all rolled up like a burrito. Mother of God. It was tied at the top by a long white streamer that seemed to give off a faint odor of nail polish remover. Hillary pulled at the top of the cylinder until she could see Sarah's white hair. Sudden fear flooded her body. Sarah was not moving, not at all, and she was a light sleeper. Hillary slid her hand down to feel for her cheek. It was cold to the touch. She felt along Sarah's jawline, trying to locate her carotid artery to feel for a pulse. Nothing.

Hillary stood rocking with terror, looking around the

room. Was someone still in it? She backed up slowly, her heart racing and her veins pulsing with ice water. The floor creaked under her bare feet and she pivoted to run down the hall to get Loretta.

"Wake up!" she whispered. "Loretta! Wake up." Hillary put her hand across Loretta's mouth and whispered close to her face, "Be quiet, don't wake Claire."

Loretta's eyes popped open and she struggled against Hillary's hand. Hillary bent near and whispered, "Claire's asleep in my bed. I need you to come with me. Be quiet."

Hillary drew back the covers and took Loretta's hand. "Shhh. Something's happened to Sarah. Come with me."

Hillary led Loretta down the hall and pointed into the room at the white bundle on the bed. Loretta's eyes widened and her jaw dropped. "No," she breathed.

"I can't feel a pulse," said Hillary. "You try. Please."

Loretta snapped on the bedside lamp and stood for a second, motionless. Then she untied the white streamer and pulled down the top of the duvet. Hillary could see Sarah's face was drained of color, her lips blue, her eyes open. Hillary stood frozen, not even breathing.

Loretta pressed her fingertips on Sarah's neck and moved them around a bit. She shook her head and stared at Hillary. "Nothing. Go down to the desk and get help."

Horrified, Hillary roused the sleeping desk clerk and told him what they'd discovered. Quietly and efficiently, as if it happened all the time, the gaunt old man went to rouse a couple younger staff members. Hillary watched as if she were in a theater where a horror show was playing. Should they be waiting for the police? Wasn't this a crime scene? She stood mute.

The three of them produced some kind of tall board from a side closet and carried it up the stairs. Hillary followed, feeling like a puppet pulled by invisible strings. The two young staffers slipped the board under Sarah.

Loretta and Hillary stared at one another in shock as they saw the white scarf around her neck dangling down like the one tied at the top of the duffel bag Bridget had been rolled up in. Like a womb, a tomb for the dead. Hillary nearly fainted and clung to Loretta as the elderly desk clerk quietly supervised his staff taking Sarah's body down the stairs.

Hillary slammed her palms against her ears, as suddenly the echo of Sarah's words came thundering into her head—if I should die, cremate me and take me back to St. Mary's, slip me in beside John.

Mother of God, she breathed. "Got to go check on Claire," she said to Loretta.

PART III

The ceremony of innocence is drowned;
The best lack all conviction, while the worst
Are full of passionate intensity.

W. B. Yeats, "The Second Coming"

CHAPTER 27

Galway, Ireland

HE HELD HER PICTURE against his chest and rubbed it as if it were a baby. What was so urgent that Dermot had her killed? What had she known that was so dangerous?

The brusque landline ring broke into his thoughts. Should he let it go to message? Suddenly he felt a need to hurry to the men's room down the hall. A woman's voice spoke aloud into the room.

"Seamus, sorry to call in the middle of the night but had to let you know that—" He picked up the handset.

"That what?" His bowels loosened. "Is this Hillary?"

"Sorry, yes." He could hear her breathing.

"What's the matter?"

"It's Sarah."

"What about her?" Silence. Jaysus, he was going to need to run down the hall now.

"She's . . ." More silence. He clenched his butt cheeks, feeling his blood pressure rising. Suddenly a different voice came on the line.

"Seamus, this is Loretta. Loretta Quinn. We met at my B&B a few days ago."

"Yes, what's wrong? Where are you?"

"It's Sarah, Hillary's friend. We're up at Connemara House, and . . .

Seamus felt a sinking in his gut at the tone of Loretta's voice. Silence. He had to prod her, "And . . . ?"

"And . . . Sarah's dead."

He sat down hard in his swivel chair. "What happened?"

"During the night, Sarah was murdered, strangled we think, anyway left wrapped in her duvet like in a cocoon."

"Jaysus," whispered Seamus.

"Hillary's nearly catatonic."

"What can I do?"

"You can phone Ed. He's away in Dublin at that summit, but he needs to know."

"Will do. What else?"

"I don't know. But . . ." she paused.

Seamus felt like waiting her out. He didn't want more bad news. Things he might have prevented if he'd not been such a . . . . Such a what? Seconds passed by, blessed seconds with no more bad news.

"But," Loretta continued, "tomorrow's little Claire's seventh birthday and we're going to have to try and put something together. Hillary is a mess right now. Come over tomorrow afternoon, if you can."

"I'll be there." He hung up the landline and ran down the hall to the men's room where he sat on the toilet for a long while.

Later, he wiped his face with pads of paper towel soaked with cold water and pushed away echoes of his brother's words calling him a loser.

Finally, he returned to his desk and sat rolling a cold cigar between his thumb and finger tips, staring out over Galway Bay. At last, he got out his throwaway phone. He called Dermot and got right through.

"When's the vote?" Dermot never spent time on social grease.

"Vote was put off until the regular time. I'm calling about a couple killings in one week. What do you know about these?"

"Murder. Better than slow death from cancer. Got to get the park open before it takes my mother, show what I've done for her. Got my guys in action. Make up for the shame laid on us."

"What shame?"

"Zip your lips on that. Build Pot O'Gold, show the positive. Your job is to stop people digging up suffering. Get that last one to fly away home."

Click.

Dermot hung up on him.

Seamus had to get a powerful scare into Hillary. Get to her to leave on schedule, with her daughter and husband still in the land of the living. What can I do? He rolled one of his Padrons between his thumb and fingers and let his mind drift over the possibilities. Maybe wipe the hard drive on Bridget's computer? Must be something awful in there, something to demolish Dermot and his plans.

Jaysus. Who've I turned into?

CHAPTER 28

CONNEMARA, IRELAND

OUTSIDE A CRACKED GLASS WINDOW, long white braids draped over a hollow globe etched with a face. Underneath this empty head, a western shirt and beaded skirt danced along the frozen grass. A hand punched out the window, grabbed at the dancer, clutched thin air.

Hillary woke with her hands tight-fisted, her mouth dry as an emery board. She pressed her curled fingers to her lips, remembering. Sarah, gone. She gazed around the room. She must have fallen asleep after she and Loretta talked to Seamus. Claire was still next to her, sleeping peacefully.

She would have to wake her and tell her about Sarah. Her heart pounding, she slid out of bed, unbuttoned her nightgown and dropped it to the floor. Stepping into the shower, she turned on the tap. How could she carry on? First Bridget, like a sister to her, killed and now Sarah, close as a mother.

Hillary held her breath and turned up the heat. The water assaulted the top of her head, drenching her hair, scalding her brains. There was no choice. She must stay in Ireland until this madman was stopped.

She stood under the hot needles, rocking back and forth on her heels in the midget-sized shower enclosure. A low keening rose from her throat and poured out like a muted bagpipe lament. After her long breath ran to its end, she pressed her forehead against the plastic lining of the shower. Sarah, like a mother to me. I who couldn't protect her. Lady bug, lady bug, your house is on fire. Take your child and fly away home. Hillary's wet hair matted tight to her scalp.

Holy Mary, Mother of God. Where are you? What was it like to witness your sacred child's agony. Where is it written how you got through the pain?

Fly home safe to California or stay here with a dark presence pushing at us, pushing invisible. Am I fit to be a mother at all? Where is Holy Mary when I need her? Her thoughts were jumbled and confused.

Hillary's years as a reporter had taught her to trust similarities, however horrible they may be: Sarah killed in the night was like Hillary's mother fleeing the country. She remembered that last time her mother tucked her in bed but was gone in the morning. She'd cried for the first month, but shut her mother out of her mind, taking refuge in her father's enveloping heart.

The water cooled. She tilted her head to rest her cheek against the hard plastic. If only I could go deaf and blind and dumb. Be locked away in this space, a woman in a stall. Not even worry about Claire.

She jerked back off the wall and told herself to focus on small things, get out of the shower, dry off, dress, go to Sarah's hotel room. Empty now of her spirit. How were they going to get her ashes back to California? Back to the grave she'd paid for, next to her husband? She had to find out how it could work.

But harder, how to tell Claire?

Hillary turned off the water. She bent down and shook her hair, grabbed it with both hands, twisted it in a long rope, hard, twisted it until her hands and her scalp hurt.

It had seemed so safe up here, away from the tourists' hustle and hard legal edges when they learned Bridget had left them that money. Seemed only right to keep their reservations, a good idea to visit this old hotel even though it was Murder Week. Claire loved hearing about it in one of her books, probably Nancy Drew, the stories about the hotel ghosts.

Hillary stepped out of the shower, dripping.

"Maaa! Maaa!" Claire burst into the bathroom. "Gran has to be taken apart."

"What?" Hillary wrapped a towel around herself.

"A man came and ... " Claire's eyes bugged out. "He said they took Gran away, that a 'topsy has to be done. She died in the night and they have to cut her apart to find out why. How could that be? Why, Maaa?" Claire stood rigid and staring up at Hillary with big eyes, like a bronze child among the statues they'd seen in Dublin of the famine victims.

Hillary felt dizzy at the sight of her daughter waiting for answers. Waiting for answers could be too dangerous now. She clutched her towel tight. They were helpless here, wedged in this space by so many sizes of pain. Yeats was right. Things fall apart.

Could she hold it together, get little Claire home safe? She felt a great wave of nausea sweep over her and swallowed two or three times to keep control. She had to get some toast into her to calm down her stomach. It hit her that she felt the same as when she'd had morning sickness. This was no time to bring new life into the world. It was time to care for the daughter she already had, to keep her out of harm's way.

CHAPTER 29

BACK AT THE QUINNS, Hillary set her tote onto the entry hall carpet and plopped down on the little bench, too tired for the few steps needed to get into her room. She felt close to dead herself, she was so exhausted.

The faint aroma of cigars drifted in from the door to the back along with Ed's deep voice. He'd phoned and let her know he'd checked in at the coroners to make sure Sarah was tended to right away. He was going to be touching bases with Seamus about the legal matters. They must be huddled in the garden.

Claire was mute as a statue, standing in front of a map of Ireland that hung on the red flocked wall of the B&B entry, unwilling or unable to talk about what happened to the woman who'd been like a grandmother to her. With a sense of doom, Hillary thought visits to a therapist might be needed when they got home.

Loretta fiddled with some paperwork behind the desk. "Guess what, Claire?" she sang out in a lilting tone.

Claire looked at her, wordless.

Loretta walked around the counter and pointed to the western shore of the island on the map. "There. Right there," she smiled.

Claire looked at the spot Loretta's finger touched. She leaned forward a few inches.

"See what it's called?" Loretta moved her finger back a half inch.

Claire's eyes widened.

"Yes, honey. It's Clare Island. Same name as you."

A faint grin crossed Claire's lips.

"And the best part," Loretta said, "is that my grandson Trevor lives there!"

Claire smiled.

"And we can go visit on a short trip by ferry boat. The island is home to a legendary pirate queen, too!"

Numb with shock over Sarah, Hillary felt grateful Loretta was tending to Claire, treating her like a princess. Claire began chattering with excitement over going to an Irish place with her name on it, although Hillary feared Claire was getting manic over that trip as a way to cover up her grief.

"We won't be too late," Loretta said.

"I might be over at Bridget's . . ." Hillary frowned. "If I can muster up the energy to see what's in her computer."

Loretta nodded and took off with Claire for their day trip. Hillary heaved a deep sigh. After the coroner's exam and release, they were going to have Sarah cremated and take her ashes back to bury at St. Mary's cemetery. It was strange she'd laid out what she wanted back before they ever left California, as if she had a premonition.

Hillary felt too tired for the foray out to Bridget's country house, too depleted to take in any more secrets.

She went to her room to lie down for a few minutes and drifted to sleep. Dreamless sleep.

After a half hour, she woke energized in a way that puzzled her, on fire to get to Bridget's computer. There were so many mysterious files stored there. She found Ed and Seamus still in the garden and got the key to Bridget's. Ed agreed to drive her out to Bridget's on his way back to Dublin, but only after he got Seamus to say he'd look in on her later.

Hillary felt the bumps on the driveway leading to the country house as bad omens, warnings. She got out of the rental and handed the house key to Ed. "You open it."

Goosebumps rose on her arms as she passed through the lounge and entered Bridget's office, a dark wood paneled space. Old books with Post-its protruding from the pages surrounded her desktop iMac, as if guarding its contents. She sensed an inexplicable energy surrounding the desk. "Do you hear anything?" She tilted her head to one side.

"What?" Ed asked. "What? Anything what?"

"A sort of humming?" She closed her eyes and cocked her head. "Not really humming almost singing like a tea kettle when the water's starting to boil. You don't hear it?"

"You mean like my tin whistle?"

"Kind of, but softer." She bent to listen near the iMac. "The computer's not on. The sound is like from an old one though—the kind with a fan inside, remember those?"

Ed held his head cocked for a long minute. "Nope. Nothing. Let's try it out."

She reached around and pressed the power button, waiting for the resounding bong she knew and loved.

The old iMac came to life, humming and whooshing for a few seconds.

She frowned at Ed. "Sounds like it's not long for this world." She typed "TeddyHeart2005" into the empty password box. Nothing happened.

She held her breath and stared at Ed.

Suddenly folders and icons popped up across a bright pink home screen.

Bridget is still connected with Teddy this way, she thought. Mother of God—together now, if there is a heaven. Wonder if Seamus knows about this? Hillary checked the browser bookmarks and then the document folder. Her jaw dropped. "She's got audio files in here," she whispered.

Ed groaned. "We should have brought a flash drive." He slapped his forehead. "Call Seamus and ask him to bring over something to copy these files onto. I hate that I'm on deck for the summit closing sessions. Damn. And then we fly away home." He kissed the top of her head. "Keep the door locked, hear? And your cell handy in case ghosts show up out here, Chickadee."

"I'll be okay. This place isn't haunted," she said.

He barked a laugh, but she caught that bloodhound look in his eyes.

She trailed him to the door and watched him back out onto the N59. Now it was time to find out what was in the stolen packet. Her heart thudded an uneven rhythm. She could call Seamus later. Now it was time to get into Bridget's secrets.

Almost afraid of what she might learn, she walked back into the kitchen, made herself a cup of tea from the loose leaf canister and stirred in sugar. It hit her that this was a simple ritual her friend could no longer do.

She sat down in Bridget's swivel chair, put down the

tea and ran her fingers through her hair, pushing it up off her temples away, releasing the dampness forming as the day warmed up.

Her thumbs rolled back and forth over her fingertips for a long minute before she set her fingers tapping at the keyboard. The desktop was crowded with folders, and one labeled "Galway Ghosts" seemed to shout out at her. She double clicked to reveal its stack of documents, shocked to see "Broome" near the top.

Broome. Ghosts. An image of her father came to mind, Gerald Broome, the least likely man on the planet to have his name linked to the paranormal. He was all facts, not a bit of the otherworldly in him, a skeptical newsman if there ever was one. Hillary had adopted the same stance toward the occult, but here in Ireland, she'd started to sense things she couldn't account for.

Now ghosts, on the screen, labeled as such by another practical and logical person, Bridget. It didn't make sense. Nonsense. Hillary again heard a faint, low humming. Where was that coming from? Was she hearing things? She looked around the room, suddenly afraid to open the "Broome" document.

She felt stuck, stuck and at the edge of paralysis, the way she had when writing a certain kind of story way back when—a story about mothers. A sort of brain freeze. But this is just reading and what does it have to do with mothers? She steepled her fingertips, pushed them against her lips and gazed at the screen for a few long seconds.

She rolled the swivel chair back from the desk to stand by the window and rub the bumpy edge of the lace curtains, staring out the window without seeing what was in front of her. In college, she'd had a sort of mental seizure when writing the story of a mother beating and burning her child to death. It froze her and in a panic under the pressure of a deadline, she'd lifted someone else's sentences and pasted them into her own story. That was the first time plagiarizing had overpowered her. She felt cold, dirty and helpless remembering it and returned to the kitchen to boil water for a refill of tea.

Afterward though, on a story about a mother down South who drowned her two boys in a river, she'd fought the urge and overcame the problem. That time.

The kettle whistled softly. She poured boiling water into her cup. Was she about to uncover a story about mothers in Bridget's Broome file?

She felt sick to her stomach as she recalled that later, on her master's project, she'd been assigned a story on mothers of terrorists. Paralysis had come back. Then plagiarism. That time, she was caught and blackmailed over her crime, a job-killing offense among journalists. Now she was a ghostwriter herself, though it had nothing to do with the unseen world—did it?

A ghostwriter. Afraid to open a folder about ghosts—family closets full of skeletons. Ghosts weren't real, not really real. But memories were—the leftover energy of people who mattered in life carried over after death. She could feel Bridget's energy in the room. She returned to the desk and opened the "Broome" file. She was going to have to dive in.

There was a photo of Grandad's mother, scrawny and pale, leaning against the doorway of a thatched cottage. Hillary felt heartbroken looking at this woman— her own great grandmother, who'd died in a tuberculosis epidemic, identified in the article as the mother of three. Three? Hillary racked her brain—there were only two—Grandad and his sister Fianna. The article contained no sources. Couldn't have been three.

The article went on to note that dying mothers had been known to kill their own babies to keep them from being put in orphanages run by nuns. As the TB epidemic raged on, Claddagh village was torched and burned to the ground by health officials. Hillary recalled the Galway Museum piece about Claddagh Village. It remained simply a story shut away in a museum, she thought, a memory replaced on the land with a plaque too small for details. A ghost town without buildings to house tormented spirits.

Hillary shuddered. Her great grandmother may have killed her own child to save her. Why hadn't Bridget told her that before? Hillary wrapped one side of her sweater tight over the other and rocked back and forth in the swivel chair. She stared at the screen, recalling the last time she'd Skyped with Bridget, and suddenly an image of her departed friend formed on the computer screen and a soft humming filled her ears.

Nonsense! She shook her head and lifted her cup to polish off the cooled liquid. She studied the tea leaves gently swaying at the bottom. What would that crazy old fortuneteller see there? She got up and walked out to the front driveway and stood in the sleety rain to clear her head.

Hillary wished she'd brought along a thumb drive—the original letters were probably part of the stolen packet. She had to hold them in her hands, feel them, old-fashioned as that might seem to some.

She would print them out for safety as soon as she finished going through the files. She gazed out at the day, turned darker than ever. For a moment, she imagined a shadow figure limping along the N59 and disappearing behind a hedgerow. She blinked rapidly to clear her sight, knowing she was under stress, hearing things lately and maybe seeing things, too. Could it be Bridget's spirit sketching in the sky what she had pictured out there on the road back in the hunger times?

Hillary turned to the bookmarked webpages. One was a column from the *Irish Times* about the property bubble bursting in 2008 and leaving behind "ghost estates" of unfinished houses abandoned by cash-strapped developers. There it was again, that word. Ghost.

She was nearly sick with nerves and started whispering file names to herself. Photos, articles, audio files. Her heart pounding in her throat, Hillary opened an audio file and there she was—Bridget in the room, same throaty voice as on Skype, her own words, quivering with sorrow: "How dare I speak of the starving as they staggered down the roadway, that same roadway I drive over every day in my bright little Audi? Did anyone come gather them up, cart them off for burial? How long were they left stiff and cold in the ditches? Were animals tempted by frozen flesh? I search for official records but only find newspaper reports, stories from priests and Quakers. Every time I drive over my driveway, I want a name to call out, a particular one of the unknown destroyed and scattered across our land in the midst of plenty—by rulers who . . . ." Bridget's voice faded into silence.

The hair on Hillary's arms stood erect, each shaft a tiny soldier waiting to hear more from her friend, alive in the room, her desire for a memorial palpable in the air—the spirit of her passion hovered over the space.

In a trance, Hillary moved on to a folder labeled "Cannibalism." One writer wrote of desperate people during food emergencies driven to it as far back as Old Testament times. Stunned, she opened a folder labeled

"Great Irish Famine of the 1840s." The first article quoted a historian commenting that "the silences surrounding cannibalism are almost deafening enough to arouse suspicion," while a professor noted in a lecture there was psychic decomposition, even down to some cases of "cannibalism in one's own family. It was, as far as we can tell, of the deranged, of those who were themselves victims, driven mad by hunger."

Driven mad. It must have driven Bridget mad to feel their agony right on her own land and not have it acknowledged. Hillary could feel a coat of sorrow slide over her, could feel the spirit of Bridget in her bones, her impetus to construct a memorial fitting for this suffering.

Hillary pushed on and found that the relative "silence" on cannibalism in Ireland during the 1840s was no proof that it did not happen. She forced herself to listen to a County Galway historian describe in a lilting brogue some accounts of cannibalism in Connemara.

Connemara. Where Sarah was killed.

Hillary stood and paced the room, the thick Persian rug grabbing at her feet. She felt nauseous and hungry at the same time. It was well past lunch and her stomach was growling but she knew not to try making a sandwich from food in Bridget's fridge. She stared out at dark green hedgerows along the N59, feeling broken in heart and soul, looking in the direction of Connemara.

Connemara, she thought, where that awful old man told Sarah's fortune, and they found her strangled the same night and cocooned in her duvet. Connemara was not far from Tuam, the site for the proposed theme park. Also, the unwed mothers' home was nearby. How calloused could a developer be to build over mass graves? To build a gaudy fun-land park, trying to appeal to rich American tourists with sentimental St. Patrick's Day green beer connections.

Hillary knew it was true that most Irish Americans yearned to believe in the fun aspects of being Irish and let the bad times disappear under the peat bogs, depleted as they were still cut into squares, dried and used as fuel by the Irish people of today.

Hillary stood and paced the floor. Suddenly her belly began bucking and she ran to the toilet, overcome with long, dry heaves. She had to sit on the edge of the tub for some time, gasping and struggling to breathe.

When she felt better, she poked around in the kitchen and found saltines in a cupboard. She nibbled a couple of them until her stomach and her nerves quieted down. Then she forced herself back to the computer.

A Dublin College professor described a documented report involving a John Connolly in the West of Ireland who came before the court on theft charges.

Connolly? Could this be an ancestor of Dermot Connolly's? Near the site of his proposed theme park? Hillary recalled the Quinn's letter to the editor accusing the developer of cannibalizing the Irish culture in his theme park plans, of being an animal that feeds on flesh of its own species.

Hillary read on. Connolly had been convicted of stealing sheep and sentenced to three months hard labor, since "an end should be put to such practices or no man's property could be safe." That punishment had prompted a local judge to testify that the prisoner and his family were starving when this crime was committed. One of Connolly's children had died and the judge had been informed that the famished mother ate part of its legs and feet after its death. The judge had had the body exhumed and found nothing but the bones remained of the child's legs and feet. A thrill of horror filled the court at this news. There was deep silence for several minutes, and many a tear trickled down the cheeks of those present. Even the court wept, and John Connolly was set free.

Bridget's grandfather clock sounded eight heavy bongs. Hillary got up, realizing dusk was beginning to gather. She paced the office. Had Bridget shared this Connolly story with Seamus? With anyone? Could that story be connected to Dermot Connolly, the developer? Is that the pressure Bridget had on him?

Hillary heard a rattle at the front door and held her breath. Had she locked the door?

CHAPTER 30

THE COUNTRY HOUSE, IRELAND

"HALLO?" Hillary recognized the voice. Seamus. She ran into the living room.

"Jaysus. What's on the porch?" he yelled through the open door.

She hadn't locked it. On the porch beside him sat a stack of papers burned nearly beyond recognition.

But she knew.

Breathing hard, she pulled her cell out and called Ed but got no answer. She left a voice mail to call back. She didn't want to disturb the papers, fragile and trembling in a fresh breeze rising after the rain. She dashed in and grabbed a towel from the linen closet to lay over the stack of ashy pages, to stop them from being blown away.

"The packet," she whispered. "Someone left it there. Bridget's papers. All burnt." She stared at Seamus. "I'm finding copies in the computer and will print them out."

He frowned. "I feel bad I've had to be gone all day on business. I've come to rescue you from your research," he said. "I think that was what got my Bridget killed—what she knew."

"She never shared it with you?" Hillary sat in the lounge, feeling drained.

"I begged her to, but she said she wanted to protect me. Imagine!" He sat across the coffee table from Hillary and slumped back into the chair. "Protect me," he repeated. He looked at Hillary. "And now here you are, vulnerable as she was. How bad is it?"

Hillary didn't know what to say. She stood and walked to the front window to check for cars and passersby. She could see no one. "It's not just my family, it's looking back to all the families here. Maybe even that developer's, Connolly." She pointed to one of the wall hangings and read it aloud. " 'People will not look forward to posterity, who never look backward to their ancestors.' That says it all, what she was working for." She faced Seamus. "It's more grisly than I dreamed," she whispered.

"That settles it," he said, going out the front door. He came back into the house holding a CD case.

She followed him into the office. "What are you doing?"

"I'm going to make a backup of her files." He slid a CD into Bridget's drive slot and hit a few keys as software windows opened. Hillary could hear a faint humming again.

"Should have done that a long time ago!" He stood tall.

Hillary felt her shoulders slump with relief. Now she wouldn't be the only one alive to carry the burden of this knowledge.

"Let's have a drink," he said, marching into the kitchen. He bent down, opened Bridget's liquor cabinet and pulled out a bottle of Jameson. He waved it in her direction. "Rocks or not?"

Hillary was astonished to see an aura form around the man. Her spirit stiffened. A sudden chill ran down her spine. Was Bridget sending her a warning from the beyond? She discovered her bold interviewer's mind, alive and throbbing beneath her sorrow. "What do you know about Dermot and his family here in Ireland?"

"He never said much. He was obsessed with his mother, who left here long ago for Hollywood with his father." He got out a couple glasses from Bridget's cupboard and yanked an ice tray from her tiny freezer compartment. "His da abandoned them when Dermot was a baby and they never heard from him again. Some kind of actor, a sort of ne'er-do-well."

Hillary felt stabbed in the heart. Abandoned by his father—what could that lead to?

Seamus went into the service porch and returned with a bottle of 7 Up. "J and Seven?"

She nodded and watched him pour her an inch of whiskey and top it off with 7 Up. He placed a couple ice cubes into the glass, handed it to her, poured himself a Jameson neat and raised his glass to clink against hers. "Sláinte chuig na fir, agus go mairfidh na mná go deo," he said. She frowned at him. "It means 'Health to the men, and may the women live forever.' " His blue eyes brimmed with unspilt tears.

She relaxed from her suspicions. Seamus really did love Bridget. She sipped her drink slowly, letting its magic work, but felt guilty in case she might be pregnant. She'd just have one. "Well, why didn't the Garda take Bridget's computer as evidence?"

"They were never told what she was up to. I figured it was better that way since the police bung things up, know what I mean? Sometimes. No offense to your husband."

Hillary flashed on the fact that it had taken Ed more than a dozen years to solve the case of his daughter's drive-by shooting, back when he was with his first wife. "Yes, but they do their best." She felt tired to the bone. Too tired to talk. She sat silent, sipping her drink, listening to a faint ringing in her ears.

"You should take your daughter and go home." He stepped close to her, so close she could smell the clean scent of his skin. "I can help you forget this horrible vacation." He rubbed her shoulder.

"What?" Was he coming on to her? Hillary shook her head. But Bridget had trusted him, so why shouldn't she?

He drained his drink and looked at her with a question in his blue eyes.

"I can't forget what Bridget wanted me to know." She took her last swallow and held out her empty glass. "One more and back to work." She wasn't about to be sharing her Irish honeymoon with another man. "But make mine straight 7 Up this time." They were on the same side, weren't they?

"Best for you to leave justice to the Garda, get on back to safe and sunny California," he said.

By now it was almost dark and they hadn't turned on any lights. Seamus made them another drink and was handing Hillary hers when there came a rattling sound from the front door.

"Shhh," Seamus said. He set his drink on the counter and tiptoed out of the kitchen. Hillary followed, drink in hand. Over at the window, shadows from the trees danced against the lace curtains. It reminded Hillary of an old black and white cartoon playing across her field of vision, like a Halloween light show of ghosts and skeletons. She shook her head. What nonsense! She

231

walked closer to the window and pulled aside the lace panel.

"It's just the wind," Hillary said, forcing a laugh and sitting down in one of the Victorian sofas in the lounge.

"I'm going to check on the downloading," said Seamus and went into Bridget's office.

On the coffee table sat the *Irish Times* Hillary'd picked up from the driveway. There it lay, rubber band still wrapped around it. No doll outside today. Where were those tiny ghosts? Seemed almost like voodoo figures from the Caribbean. Hillary got Bridget's letter out from her pocket and double checked. Yes. She'd saved the dolls in a pillowcase up in a cupboard in her service porch.

Hillary walked through the house to the porch and noticed the washer and dryer were the best brands, the ones Liam said Loretta couldn't afford. It hit Hillary that due to Bridget's generosity, she and Ed were now rich. Remarkably rich. But money couldn't bring back the dead.

She looked around. Some boxes were stacked on shelves but they were all empty—Bridget was a saver, for sure. Near the washer and dryer were two cupboards, and she opened the lower one—nothing but a bottle of Fairy liquid detergent, a stack of cloth rags, a basket of shoe polish in various colors and some loose vacuum cleaner tools.

She reached up to the cupboard above the washer. There it was. A white pillowcase, twisted in the middle into a bundle. She gathered her courage, heart pounding, and lifted the bundle off the shelf. As she stood with it swaying gently from her fist, she heard a shaking sound coming from the other end of the house, followed by a thumping. She froze.

It was Claire clumping through the house shouting "Maaa, Maaa, come out wherever you are!" She burst into the small space and smiled up at her mother, revealing an empty space in her grin. "My tooth fell out over on Clare Island! Loretta said the Irish tooth fairies leave a shiny €2 coin." She smiled with her teeth clenched together, poking a bit of her tongue through the now empty space, then said, "I hope they come see me even though I'm not an Irish kid." She grinned up at Loretta, who'd followed her in.

"Well, you really are an Irish girl," Hillary said. "Your great grandfather was born not more than five miles from here."

"You left the door unlocked," said Loretta. Hillary gasped and shook her head. Where were her wits anymore?

Claire again stuck her tongue through the new empty space. "What's in the bag, Maaa?" She patted at the lumpy pillowcase.

"Let's take it out to the dining room and have a look," Hillary said, nodding at Loretta and Seamus who had followed Claire back into the service porch. Hillary noted a satisfied look on his face.

"Backup going okay?"

Seamus laughed and nodded. "Taking care of everything."

They trooped into Bridget's dining room. Hillary stood at the head of the table and set the white bundle down on a placemat. She folded the hem of the pillowcase down a few times. Loretta, Seamus and Claire stood attentively around the table.

Hillary picked up one of the tiny figures and held it by its rubber-banded neck, its little round head at the top, its draped body floating down in the four points of the handkerchief it was made from. She wiggled it a bit so that it appeared to dance in the air.

"How cute! A little doll, a little Halloween doll." Claire turned to Seamus. "Do you have Halloween over here?"

Seamus laughed a deep chuckle. "Sure, it just about started over here, didn't you know, Rapunzel my dear?"

Claire smiled and patted her blond braids.

"We call it Samhain, 'All Hallowtide' or," Seamus let out a low chuckle, "the 'Feast of the Dead', when the departed come back to this world. But it's two months away so no need to worry now. You'll be going home soon, where you're nice and safe."

Hillary felt a chill up the back of her neck. What was it about this man?

Claire reached over and took a doll into each hand. Holding them near the tabletop, she put them into a drama. Bowing one to the other, she said in a deep cartoon voice, "Get out here tonight and practice your trick or treating, you hear me?"

"No, no. I'm afraid to go up to those scary houses!" Claire cried in a high voice for the tiny figure on the right. "You go for me."

On and on, Claire animated the little dolls, their rolled handkerchief hems dusting the table top as they moved around in her drama.

"They need faces, Maaa." Claire stopped the action and looked at Hillary, who had taken out another half dozen figures from the pillowcase, so that it was nearly empty.

"We need to leave them as is for a bit, Princess," said Hillary.

"Why, Maaa? Why?" Claire looked worried, pushing out her bottom lip.

"Well, these are part of a mystery we are trying to solve."

"Mystery? Can I help?"

"You probably need to put them back in the pillow-case," said Seamus. "This mystery will be investigated by the Garda."

Claire looked from her mother to Seamus and back. Her thin shoulders slumped and she pushed the two dolls in her mother's direction. "I like 'em, these little ghosty dolls. Can we get 'em back from the police when they're done? Can I give 'em faces?"

Faces, thought Hillary. She held open the pillowcase for her daughter to drop the dolls into. What happens, she wondered, when ghosts have faces?

Loretta stood. "Let's go start in on your birthday cake." She reached out her hand and Claire jumped up and took it, pulling Loretta towards the front door.

"Don't disturb the towel on the front steps," Hillary called out.

"What's in there?" asked Loretta as Claire ran ahead out to the car.

"A stack of ashes, all that's left of Bridget's packet . . . ." Hillary's heart nearly stopped. She felt faint and reached to steady herself against the door jam. "Ashes . . . all that's left of her, too," she whispered.

Loretta gave her a hug and then hurried out to her car where Claire had already jumped into the back seat.

Hillary turned to see Seamus standing behind her, his jaw dropped open. "Ashes," he said. "I can't believe it."

"She wants them scattered in front near her roses and along the N59," Hillary whispered.

"I can't take it," he cried, slumping into a sofa.

"You've got to man up," Hillary said.

"You don't know the worst part," he said, pounding his fist into his palm. "I just checked on the computer and . . ."

Hillary waited. What else could happen?

"And?"

"The computer is dead."

"Dead?"

"I wanted to check on the backup, but now all I get is a blank screen with a flashing question mark."

"I really have to save those papers now," she said. She searched the back porch and found a box the right size to fit the burned stack. Her fingers were charred black by the time she got the mess into the box.

"This may not be any good at all," she cried. "Now I'll have to stay on and testify at the council meeting what I read in the computer."

"You won't need to," Seamus said, "if you tell me about it. I can report to the committee."

Hillary felt her gut doing belly flops. Could she trust this man or not?

CHAPTER 31

THE OPEN FIELD, IRELAND

SEAMUS PARKED at the edge of the unmarked acreage. There they were, a couple pieces of heavy equipment, one digging up the ground, biting at the edges of an open pit, the other standing by to scoop up dirt and haul it off to a waiting lorry. Damn. Dermot must have assumed he'd get approval and jumped ahead to get started on the sly. Not that the work was quiet. The digger driver in his little cab ground the gears in chorus with the bulldozer operator gripping his control sticks. The earth gaped open like that in pictures of Nazi camps.

Seamus smelled nervous sweat pooling under his arms. Dermot could have already given the green light for another hit—clear out the last obstacle to building his cursed park his way. Thick arrogant asshole.

A hot flush bloomed through the stubble on Seamus's cheeks. His brother's slurs echoed in his mind— loser, weakling. He had to scrape up the courage to stop the devil developer. He could do it. After all, he'd been able to get away with crashing Bridget's hard drive.

He pulled his cell out, his fingers shaking and tapped in Hillary's number. "Wanted to let you know I'm working on getting Bridget's bequest to you," he said, "so you can leave on schedule."

"No rush, really." Hillary said. "In fact, I'm staying on with Claire. Ed needs to go home, but Claire's learning more here than she would in second grade." She sighed. "At least through next week. I'll go and talk in person to the council, give them stories and references that were in the computer, let them know Dermot has to face the truth, get over his false shame, and his never-apologize persona. Let his family tragedy stand as part of Bridget's museum."

Seamus felt paralyzed, his nerves shimmered hot with shame—responsible for Bridget and Sarah, too. Hillary had to get out before she was the target of that madman and whoever he was hiring to set up his kills.

"It would be a public relations catastrophe for him," Seamus countered.

"No, I think the public would admire him for it," she said.

The woman was an idealist, like his Bridget. He could feel his gut churning. He had to stop this, had to have the courage to put an end to it. What would convince Hillary to let this drop, to fly back safe to California?

"Nothing you can really do," he muttered.

"I feel responsible," she said.

"You? Why?"

"I should have come sooner, stopped her from those night walks, kept Sarah . . ." She choked up.

"How about taking those as a warning? You know, take little Claire and your copper hubby and fly away home."

238

"No. No. No. I should have been here sooner. Now I have to be Bridget's voice. Kind of like ghost writing."

Seamus felt his skin crawling. How could he get this stubborn woman to leave? Get the hell away from Dermot's madness?

"Aren't you worried for your safety?"

"I'm trained in karate and know how to use it," she said.

"What about your daughter?"

"I . . ." Hillary's voice halted. He could hear the force of her silence. That was it. He could put little Claire into grave danger—that would do the trick.

The child was in love with fairy tales and castles. A vision formed in his mind. He could get a key from Sean Mor. Get things set up ahead of time. He felt rigid with excitement. Now he had a plan to save them.

CHAPTER 32

FRIDAY MORNING, Hillary functioned like an automaton as she went through the motions of taking care of the cremations. Ed was still in Dublin and Liam drove her around town. His kindness held her together as she completed the paperwork for getting Sarah's ashes out of the country before she turned to Bridget's ashes.

The will had directed her remains be spread in front of her country house, to be mixed in with the bones of those who suffered so much. Hillary felt bogged down with sorrow and grief, heavy-hearted yet almost soothed to take the box of ashes out there and spread them along the roadside. Sorrow and grief plucked at her edges, but she could feel Bridget's spirit approving as she sprinkled the last granules from the funeral home box out among Bridget's roses of many colors.

Liam drove her back to the B&B where she found Claire helping Loretta bake a cake in the shape of the number seven for her birthday dinner. What a Godsend to have dear Loretta. She felt like part of the family now. Hillary sat with a cup of tea in the dining room, letting her mind go blank.

Seamus arrived around seven with a glittering toy princess crown for Claire and a bunch of white roses he handed to Hillary.

"Here's to milady," he said, bowing. "Sorry you'll be leavin' our lovely land so soon."

Hillary shook her head. "I meant it when I said we'll be staying, keep digging into what's going on around here. Can't keep running away from the tough stuff. With the money Bridget left me, it's the least I can do now that I don't have to ghost write for a living anymore."

"Really?" Seamus narrowed his eyes. "I thought after our chat that you'd have considered departing our misty shores for sunny California?"

"No," said Hillary. "I feel I owe it to both of them . . ." She sighed. "See if I can help solve the mystery."

"What mystery?" Claire came bouncing into the room. "Like in Nancy Drew stories?"

"Not that kind," Seamus winked at Claire, "I may have some fairy tale fun in store for a seven-year-old, before she grows too big for the Rapunzel kind."

Claire giggled and pulled her long blond hair over both shoulders, framing her face.

After dinner and cake, Seamus suggested they play Hide and Go Seek in the alleyways behind the B&B. It was the new moon so there was barely any light. Claire ran around as if she had on night goggles, being the one nobody could find. Hillary felt a glow of pride for her spunky daughter right up until it was her turn to hide again and she couldn't find her.

"Where's the birthday girl got off to?" Hillary called out to Liam.

He shook his head. "Loretta, you have a clue?"

The three of them searched in the back alleyway, but no Claire. Nor Seamus. They moved to the front yard. No white Yaris in the small parking lot. Hillary punched Seamus's number into her cell. His leave a message recording came on. "He's not answering."

Loretta ran to the van. Fastened under the windshield wiper blade was a folded sheet of paper.

Liam yanked out the note and read aloud. "We'll be playing a different game—in the tower." He looked at Hillary. "It's signed '—Rapunzel and friend.'"

"The tower? Yeats tower? That's over a half hour away," yelled Loretta. "Let's go!" She ran toward the van and shouted over her shoulder. "Liam, call the Garda!"

Hillary's stomach begin to heave. She clutched her throat and tried to swallow. What was Seamus up to?

CHAPTER 33

LORETTA BROKE SPEED RECORDS driving to the tower. As they drove through the dark woods toward the clearing, Hillary spotted Seamus's car parked outside the thatched white cottage. She jumped out of the van and stood in the shadow of the ancient tower, grateful for the headlights shining on the dirt road running past Thor Ballylee. Like a human searchlight, she scanned up and down the face of the old structure. It rose like a ghostly battleship into the night sky. No lights shone through the tiny windows, one at each of the four stories.

A cold chill shook her with force. Her veins traced icy pathways under her skin. Loretta opened the driver's door and stood looking at Hillary, as for directions.

"How can we get inside?" Hillary muttered in a stage whisper, going numb with terror. What kind of a mother was she? It was suddenly clear she and Seamus belonged to different species. She had trusted him with her brightest treasure, and now he had that treasure up in a tower of stone.

"This can't be any kind of game at all, can it?" she whispered. Seamus may be hunkered down in darkness, holding little Claire silent. That was the best scenario Hillary could hope for.

Loretta shook her head. "Sean Mor's not here with his key," she said. She walked to the back of the van and pulled out what looked like an axe. Hillary gasped.

"Just in case," said Loretta. "Let's get to it." She led the way to the cottage, axe hanging at her side, and tested the knob of the old wooden door.

Hillary stood waiting, barely breathing.

"It's open," Loretta whispered. "Seamus, that devil must have got the key from Sean Mor." She pushed the door, stepped in and turned to motion Hillary into the dark and musty room. "I'll stand guard here, get Liam on the phone, make sure he sent help. I'm at the ready to whisk you and Claire to safety."

Hillary put her hand up against the doorframe to steady herself as she stepped into the dank interior. "How do I find them?"

Loretta pointed in the direction of the tower. "Through that archway."

Hillary shivered in the dampness. "Can you come?"

"The stairwell is narrow. You can do it. Go up the stone steps . . ." Hillary could hear Loretta's key ring jingling. After a few seconds, Loretta turned on a tiny penlight and pressed it into Hillary's hand. "Use this when you need it. I'll follow if I can."

Hillary clenched her teeth and turned in the direction of the tower, wishing there were more of a moon, but not even a sliver of light showed through the window at the right of the door. She pressed the flashlight's tiny *on* button as she placed one foot then two over the threshold and onto the damp stone floor of the tower. She inhaled and yelled as loud as she could, "Seamus! Where are you?"

Silence. Then in deep tones: "Claire and I are playing up here."

"Where?" She couldn't hear her own voice. She must have been simply thinking it. She lifted her chest and forced out a resounding tone. "Where? Are you both on the same floor?" She froze in place, feeling an uncanny breeze on her cheeks, fearful of venturing further into the ground floor of the tower.

His low chuckle felt like it gathered around her face. "Just take the stairs."

Then giggles from her daughter. Hillary's blood stood still in her veins. She held her breath and listened. Nothing. "I don't see the stairs. Can't you turn on some lights?"

Quicker response. "But that would spoil the game, wouldn't it Claire?"

Faint snickering. "Maaa, I told Seamus you would show up to play Princess in the Tower."

Hillary aimed the penlight's pale beam around the room. She spotted the spiral stairway in the corner and moved toward it, calling up the opening: "Claire, honey, tell me where you are."

"Here's some hints. We're in one of the four floors. Which floor has a window tall enough to let down her hair from?" Low chuckles. "Hmmm?"

Hillary knew he was playing like a villain from a movie.

"Her strawberry blond hair like Yeats' little boy's hair. Can you see Michael sitting by the window? It's his birthday today, too. August 22." Laughter.

Hillary took a step on the stairs, reaching out to steady herself against the clammy stone wall. "Claire, do you know which floor you're on?"

"Pretend you're blindfolded, Maaa."

"Claire, Loretta and I are here to take you home. It's way past your bedtime."

Her daughter's voice took on a whine. "It's not that late, Maaa."

Seamus voice boomed down the stairwell. "Claire is having fun with Yeats' story, Hillary. She's a brave princess, aren't you Claire? Help out the boy in the tower. Help his ghost rest in peace. Give him a wave when we get to the roof. He'll fly out the window and up to greet you."

Hillary felt for the stone wall and lifted her foot, one after another onto the irregular wedges of steps, until she reached the next floor. "Are you here? Is this high enough? Did you count the steps as you went up the stairs?"

Nothing.

"Claire?" Hillary listened hard. Seamus's gravelly singsong reached her: "We were singing, not counting, weren't we, Claire, my little love?"

"I've come up fourteen steps, Claire, and I'm on a flat floor now. There's no moon so I can't see." Hillary waited, listening.

"Maaa, you are such a fraidy cat!" Giggles.

Hillary kept climbing. Her palm, pushed up against the stone wall, had gone numb, the tiny penlight like a shard of ice banged against her thin cotton sleeve. "The next steps are bringing me up into what feels like a smaller room."

Silence in the dark cold tower.

Suddenly the rough tones of Seamus's voice rang down. "The red-headed boy was only a ghost, not real, little Claire, so not to worry." His demented laugh seemed to stimulate Claire's snickers. "Besides, he already flew out the window, to climb up and kiss you

246

when you let down your long hair."

Hillary felt a cobwebby draft against her neck. "I hear your voice, getting louder."

"You're getting warm." Seamus let out a yowl. Hillary stumbled and scraped her shin against a jagged stone step. She bent to grab at her leg in the darkness. Seamus was yelling, his voice rushing down from the top floor of the tower. "Look at that lovely dark water, Claire. Want to go for a midnight swim? I'll let you down by your long hair."

"It's not that long, silly." Claire's voice sounded light and easy, fainter and soft now. How much more would it take for her grasp the danger?

"Okay," Hillary sang out, "I've got just fourteen more steps to reach you and win the game."

"It's not that kind of game," breathed Seamus in a stage whisper. He'd turned to call back down the steps. "It's not a game anyone can win."

Panting, Hillary stepped up from the dim stairwell onto the rough slabs of the tower roof. The moon peeked out from under its thick cloud cover. Seamus stood at the edge, stern-faced and clutching a thick hunk of Claire's hair in one hand. "You'll only win if you promise to fly away home."

The huffing and puffing behind her ceased. Hillary held her breath and listened. Loretta must have made it onto the roof. Hillary glanced back, relieved to see her clutching the axe.

Hillary stared at Seamus, hoping he would say something. Clearly it was Claire's hair he was gripping. There was no sound nor movement coming from below the roof railing, four stories above the river. He must have knocked her out. Or drugged her. He stood rigid as a statue as if under some kind of spell.

247

Hillary didn't dare break the silence of the night. She sidled over to the short wall and leaned over. There was Claire hanging by her long blond hair from the tower rooftop. She made no sign of life, hanging still and small, like a sleeping toddler. Water flowed by down below, dark water like in dreams.

She could feel the cold steel of the axe head as Loretta pressed it into her back. The voice of Seamus boomed out of the night like the devil himself roaring up from the deeps. "You must go home. Leave this land. Take your girl and fly home. Or she will belong to the dark Irish waters."

"You can't mean that, Seamus. Bridget trusted you."

"She never knew," he started choking on his words, "how far I'd fallen into the 'ould boy's' pockets—the devil himself bought me out."

"Bridget trusted you and so do I," said Hillary. "Bring my girl back over, do it now." She ran toward him.

Seamus began keening in a high voice. "The ceremony of her is about to be drowned, can't you hear the young boy calling?"

Hillary froze. He was going off his rocker, blending Yeats with songs of lament.

"His boy's singing to us up from the window below." Seamus began laughing. "Can't ya see his ghost drifting up? It's his birthday today, ya know! Same as your little princess." He began teetering from side to side. "Worst bein' full of passionate intensity, for sure—top of the worst being Dermot from your own California," he shrieked. "While, I who tried to be the best lack all . . ." His voice faded to a whisper. ". . . lack all of everything." A sob erupted from his throat. He waved his fistful of blond hair around in a wide circle and stared straight at Hillary.

"Promise you'll take her on home!" he screamed as he pulled Claire up over onto the roof and at the same time, as if a living counterweight, flung himself over the edge.

Hillary grabbed Claire and folded her into her arms, limp little Claire. She was silent with closed eyes. But she was breathing.

Loretta let the axe drop to her side. "He's a goner, for sure," she called out. "Even if the thatched roof breaks his fall, he won't make it to heaven, that one."

With Claire clutched to her breast, Hillary made her way to the top of the steep stairwell. Leaning against the outer stone wall for support, she carried the light frame of her daughter down the spiral stairway.

From a distance, she could hear the waa waa waa of sirens.

CHAPTER 34

GALWAY, IRELAND

CLAIRE SAT CUDDLED on Hillary's lap in the sunny breakfast room. Every few minutes she leaned forward for a sip of chamomile tea sweetened with milk and honey. Hillary could feel each cell in her body swell with relief that her small daughter was all right, and that she still fit on her lap. She rocked slowly in the chair as she listened to her husband.

Ed was explaining what he and the Garda had ferreted out from interviewing the ambulance attendant. It seems Seamus had survived. The straw of the cottage roof broke his fall, and he asked for a priest in the moments before they reached the emergency room.

"He wanted to get it off his chest," Ed said. "He claimed the Garda should pick up Dermot, said the American developer was the greedy mind at work behind the two murders, and more." Ed shook his head. "Seamus insisted Dermot was desperate to hide the fact that one of his ancestors had literally cannibalized her own son, when she was driven mad from the great hunger."

Hillary felt her hackles rise at the word cannibal—

same as in Bridget's computer!

"He knew that horror would ruin the theme park proposal if it got out, so he had to silence Bridget and then try to scare you off her computer records—get you to leave the country."

Hillary nodded. It finally made some sense. Of a horrid sort.

"Dermot of course is beyond Irish law though they will try to get him, but the irony for him is that his own Irish father was the actual killer hired by some middle man." Ed shook his head. "Dermot's dropping his proposal for the theme park. His father Denis has been arrested, along with a man named Kane, some respectable accountant who was the go-between."

Loretta refilled the tea cups and went to take Liam's hand in hers. "We will be reforming Bridget's All-Irish committee to keep up the pressure against outside developers, work to champion our authentic tourist attractions," said Loretta.

Hillary sighed. "I'll leave a good bit of funding to patch up Thoor Ballylee," she said. "That ghost of Yeats' boy whispered the right words at the right time." Or some kind of spirits on their side. Bridget's? Sarah's? From the great mystery?

It was time to go home.

EPILOGUE

LODI VINEYARD, CALIFORNIA

HILLARY KISSED ED GOODBYE and waved at his departing unmarked. She'd been right—she could trust him with everything. They'd held a service at St. Mary's in Sacramento and placed Sarah's ashes in next to her darling husband's. Now every fall there'd be a Day of the Dead parade to remember them by.

Life was moving on to a new normal. Gilhooley's was throwing a Welcome Back party for them later that week. Roger'd run a bylined story in *The Acorn*, calling Hillary a "shero." She was no longer simply his ghost writer but the subject of the news.

She turned to watch Claire step slowly across the creaky old back porch, looking in the direction of Sarah's cottage. "Sarah won't be there anymore," said Claire.

"No, honey." Hillary held her breath. There was no sound in the bright morning except a sudden squeak as Claire placed one foot down onto the weathered wooden step. She turned to look at Hillary.

"Can we go and light one of her candles? Maybe the yellow rose is still there."

"She would love that," Hillary said, aching in this ongoing grief. "I've got her key with mine. Let me go in and get it."

When she got back to the porch, Claire had made her way down to the dirt patch alongside the house, the yellow labs Daisy and Rufus leaping with joy beside her. She stood fingering the edges of petals on the roses. "I won't stick myself this time, Mom," she said. "Now I know where the thorns are hiding."

Once inside the cottage, Claire picked up the rose she'd taken to Sarah a few weeks before. It was dried now but still a bright color. "Yellow. It was her favorite."

Hillary nodded, blinking back tears.

"Yellow, like my hair." She pulled off her scrunchie and shook out her long hair. "I want to have it cut and give it for wigs for children with cancer. I'll tell them it was Grannie Sarah's idea." Claire thrust out her chin. "Let's go measure it, Mom. It's way more than ten inches, don't you think?" She was out the door, on her way back to the big house.

Hillary couldn't stop tears from rolling down her cheeks.

She figured next year she'd take her on a trip to Roratonga to meet her grandmother face to face. If that's where Hillary's mother still was. Claire would soon be mature enough to handle the complexities. She'd dealt so well with the sad chaos their vacation had turned into.

Now Hillary had no choice. She had to go find her mother, her blood mother, and ask her why. Why did she abandon her?

How in the world could Hillary ever forgive her? What did it take to learn to forgive? It hit her she need-ed a change of perspective. She'd been living in the shoes of her ten-year-old self but that was then. This was now, and she was forty-four and pregnant with another child.

Wordsworth's line, "The Child is father of the Man," flashed across her mind. She was blessed to have Ed as the father of her children. Suddenly she saw Claire as mother of the woman, choosing to have her hair cut demonstrating her moral courage at seven, the age of reason in the Catholic church.

It hit Hillary. She'd been bound by her own childhood memories but released by her child's actions—she must be good enough after all, to have mothered a girl like Claire. Good enough now to go looking for her own mother. Now that she knew where she came from on her father's side. On her Irish side. What was on her mother's side?

It was time to find out.

THE END

ACKNOWLEDGMENTS

For the seed idea of *House of Eire*, I am indebted to my daughter Julie who asked me to write about ghosts and to my son Mike for recommending the documentary film *You've Been Trumped*, which reveals an instance of the grievous impact of greedy businessmen on the little people.

Hearing my mother sing "Galway Bay" over the years put a yearning in my heart to go across the sea to Ireland, and I'm grateful to have visited there three times as a foundation for this novel. Even though some of the sad and scary parts of Eire show up in my book, I deeply love it and am thrilled at its new prosperity while praying the old times and the links to the world beyond the five senses continue to get the respect they deserve, as so well exemplified by groups such as

Yeats Thoor Ballylee Society
https://yeatsthoorballylee.org/
Christine Valters Paintner's Abbey of the Arts
http://abbeyofthearts.com/

Big hugs to my cheerleaders over the many long months it's taken to bring *House of Eire* to publication: Karen, Jan, Kay, Nancy, Leslie and Bonnie. I could not have made it without the feedback from Michele, Linda, Pam and Sherry, my writing buddies in Capitol Crimes, Sacramento chapter, Sisters in Crime, and from Gold Country Writers novel critique authors Ann, Sharyn and Mary Helen.

Two years in the Stanford Online Novel Certificate Program were mind-bending and opening, especially the input from Joshua Mohr and Ammi Keller—both inspiring writers and teachers. Gratitude to beta readers Jacki, Reene, Julie and Janet Ann. Copy editor Suzanne Murphy and formatter R.M. ArceJaeger were wonderfully professional to work with.

I am grateful to you, my reader, and eager to hear what you think about *House of Eire*. Please contact me at www.junegillam.com or tweet me @junegillam or just post to my Facebook page: June Augusta Gillam. Or, find me on Goodreads. I hope to see you in the next and final book of the series, as well: *House of Hoops*—Hillary in a basketball setting where some folks play foul for a living.

ABOUT THE AUTHOR

June Gillam is a novelist, poet, and writing teacher at San Joaquin Delta College. She explores social issues through her characters who suffer from powerful forces nearly too big to handle. To date, her Hillary Broome series has explored the

- effects of superstores on a small market owner, in *House of Cuts*
- impact of patriarchy on a woman in business, in *House of Dads*
- villainy of a theme park developer in Ireland, in *House of Eire*

Her poems have been published in outlets such as Amherst Artists & Writers *Peregrine Journal* and her chapbook *So Sweet Against Your Teeth*, her short stories in venues such as *Metal Scratches and America's Intercultural Magazine*. She can be reached at www.junegillam.com or tweeted @junegillam or contacted on her Facebook page: June Augusta Gillam.

Made in the USA
Las Vegas, NV
09 September 2021